LONG TIME COMPANION

First Edition

Published by The Nazca Plains Corporation
Las Vegas, Nevada
2012

ISBN: 978-1-61098-207-8
Ebook ISBN: 978-1-61098-208-5

Published by
The Nazca Plains Corporation ®
4640 Paradise Rd, Suite 141
Las Vegas NV 89109-8000

PUBLISHER'S NOTE
Long Time Companion is a work of fiction created wholly by Hank Brooks' imagination. All characters are fictional and any resemblance to any persons living or deceased is purely by accident. No portion of this book reflects any real person or events.

Model Cover Photos, Purmar
Art Director, Blake Stephens

To my long time companion.

LONG TIME COMPANION

First Edition

Hank Brooks

CONTENTS

CONTENTS CONTINUED

PROLOGUE

Evan Morrissey's obituary read as follows:

Morrisey, Evan, 88, passed quietly in his sleep, Sunday, May 8. He is survived by his longtime companion, Adam Langston of Ft. Lauderdale, FL, and a brother, Edward, of Long Island, NY. He will be laid to rest at Holy Cross Cemetery. A memorial service will be held at Moore Funeral Home at 10 AM on Wednesday, May 11.

"That's it?" Adam thought. "After a lifetime of love, service to his community, and uncountable good deeds, his life is summed up in 50 short words." Adam turned his head into his pillow and wept silently. His only consolation lay in the sure certainty, that at 83, he would probably be reunited with Evan very shortly. Involuntarily his hand reached out to touch Evan, only to be met by an empty, rather cold pillow.

Adam didn't know how he would survive the funeral or even get to the funeral home. He didn't feel capable of driving himself at the moment. His only family, two younger brothers and Evan's brother, lived thousands of miles away and had already informed him that they could not possibly make the funeral. He had thought of asking the executive director of the assisted living facility for some help, but Steve Baron knew that Adam and Evan were a gay couple and he detested them. He did not hide his feelings, and Adam was loathe to ask him for further assistance.

There was a gentle knock on the door. Adam got out of bed and went to open the door. "Just a minute," he said when he realized that he was totally naked. He and Evan never wore anything in their cozy little apartment. He put on a bath robe and opened the door. It was Jamie Gordon, his next door neighbor.

Jamie was a mere boy as far as Adam and Evan were concerned. He was only 67 when he took up residence at The Sunnydale House just a year ago. His wife had passed away two years before that. They never had any children, and Jamie had grown tired of living alone. He was straight, and it didn't bother him one iota that his next door neighbors were gay. He took the older men under his wing, and drove them to shopping and doctor appointments so that they didn't have to wait for, and be slaves to, the bus provided by the facility. When they grew tired of eating every meal at Sunnydale the three of them went to restaurants together.

"I just wanted to tell you that I'll drive Wednesday to the Funeral Home. Just don't worry about a thing," Jamie said. "I don't wish to get personal, but if you need money or anything, I'd be glad to lend you some."

"Oh, Jamie. You are so kind," Adam sobbed. "We both pre-arranged our funerals so most of the costs are covered. Thank you so much for offering."

"You look so tired man. I think you should really get some rest. I'll come and get you when it's time for dinner. You get into bed," Jamie advised, "and I'll see you later." He left and closed the door softly behind him.

Adam removed his robe, and climbed back into bed. The sheets suddenly felt cold and he pulled up the blanket that was at the foot of the bed. He covered himself and tried to rid his mind of his terrible grief, hoping perhaps that he might be lucky and get a few hours of much needed sleep. Try as he might, he could not erase his memories of the past and sleep was a long time in coming.

CHAPTER ONE

The year was 1946. The war had recently ended, and Adam Langston was looking forward to his high school graduation. He lived in New Brunswick, NJ, about forty-five minutes to Newark and an hour to Manhattan by train, slightly longer by bus. He had just narrowly missed being conscripted for the war, and now enjoyed a further student deferment.

All of his kin had attended Rutgers University, but Adam told his parents that he wanted to go to New York University and get out of their home town for a while. They were totally opposed, but Adam was so adamant that they finally consented. With the help of a small scholarship, Adam was admitted to NYU. The University was giving priority to returning veterans and he was one of the few non-veterans admitted that year. Adam was unable to tell his parents the real reason he so wanted to get out of his provincial surroundings.

Adam was homosexual. The word gay was not yet in his vocabulary. Indeed, it might not have been invented yet. He felt that Manhattan's urban setting and famed Greenwich Village might be more to his liking than Rutgers sleepy campus. NYU's downtown campus was located adjacent to Greenwich Village.

He had first acted on his passions when he was a sixteen year old junior in high school. Actually he was seduced. Early one Saturday morning his parents had permitted him to visit his favorite uncle in Manhattan. Uncle Stan was only eight years older than Adam and Adam idolized him. He had been wounded in the war, and had received an early discharge from the army. He had secured a good job in Manhattan just before he married. Now Stan and his bride lived on the upper west side, a short bus ride to his office.

After getting off the train at Pennsylvania Station, Adam had to take a subway train uptown, and then back again to catch the return ride. He had lunch with his uncle and new aunt and left them about two o'clock. He entered the subway car, and sat down in an empty seat. Even before the train came to the first stop, a handsome young man in his early twenties smiled at Adam and sat down next to him. No sooner did he sit down (very close to the young boy) he put his hand on Adam's knee.

Adam was shocked and thought he should run, but he was afraid to. The handsome young man's hand crept up Adam's thigh and reached its target. He squeezed gently on Adam's growing cock. Adam did not know what to do and simply stared into space. This was as close to his fantasies as reality had ever taken him. Adam allowed the man to fondle him, more out of fear than desire.

Conquering his fears, Adam placed his hand on the young man's knee, but went no further. The man leaned over and whispered in Adam's ear, "I live in The Village. Why don't you come for a visit and I'll see to it that we both have a good time?"

The Village: Greenwich Village. Adam knew that area of Manhattan was a Mecca for homosexuals. He was now torn between desire and fear. He *feared* that *desire* was going to win.

"Do you have a phone?" he asked. That was a legitimate question. The effects of the war had not yet ended. Telephones were a top priority and difficult to obtain. There were long waiting lists. Pregnant women and households with babies had first priority. A healthy young, single man might not yet have gotten a phone.

"Yes," the man answered. "Why do you ask?"

"I'll have to call my folks, and let them know that I'll be late. I don't want them to worry."

"Sure. That'll be fine," he answered.

"It's a long distance call," Adam informed him.

"Still not a problem. What's your name kid?"

"Adam. What's yours?"

"Just call me Eve!"

That afternoon Eve introduced Adam to the joys of gay sex. Adam could not get enough. Eve went down on him immediately after they undressed. The moment Adam felt Eve's tongue caressing his cock, he nearly swooned and frightened his host. He came quickly and told Eve he wanted to reciprocate. Eve came almost as quickly as Adam. Adam never lost his erection and Eve instructed him in how to fuck. Adam entered Eve easily, and Eve informed him that he was a bottom. That was the first time Adam had heard that expression. Notwithstanding his preference, Eve fucked Adam to give him the experience. He was delighted to have snared a virgin. That afternoon Adam came three times to Eve's twice. No matter, both men knew that they would never see each other again. It was Adam's only homosexual encounter until the day he met Evan.

Evan Morrissey was a hardened foot soldier, a veteran of the Battle of the Bulge. He had not had good grades in high school, but his military status helped him gain admission to NYU. At orientation, he sat right behind Adam, and his dorm room was five doors down from Adam's. They were actually in the same English Lit class. The professor assigned his students alphabetically to help him learn their names quickly. He seated Adam Langston at the end of one row, then Lindstrom, Logan, Mancuso, Markowitz, and finally Morrissey. They were in the third row at opposite ends of the room and never spoke to each other. They were hardly aware of each other's existence. After two weeks, they happened to pass each other in the hallway and nodded to each other in slight recognition.

Four weeks into the semester, Adam finally worked up the courage to make the long anticipated voyage to Greenwich Village. He was actually walking distance from what he perceived would be Nirvana. He hoped that he could stop jacking off and have real sex. He thought back to Eve and desired what he could now barely remember. He had been too scared at the time to note where the man lived or to get his real name or he would most certainly have tried to contact him.

It was a late September Friday evening. The temperature was hovering in the high sixties. It was a good evening for a walk. Adam put on a light cardigan sweater over his shirt, took a deep breath and started out to The Village. Upon entering the heart of The Village, he was at a loss where to go. He wandered up and down the streets with their quaint stores, sex shops and restaurants. He passed several bars, but they were all occupied by men and women. In many of them he found mixed couples being somewhat intimate and he passed those by. Finally he came upon a likely looking bar. It was called The Male Room, and that removed all doubt. Adam walked right by it. He was afraid to go in. His knees were literally shaking.

As had happened to him once before, his desire overcame his fear. He returned to the bar and went in. The place was dimly lit. Soft music was playing and he could see men dancing together, holding tight, and rubbing their bodies together. This was a sight he had never seen before except at Greek and Jewish weddings, but those were always circle dances. There was no real contact like he was witnessing right now.

Looking around he spotted the bar. There was an empty seat at one end and he quickly occupied it. New York State required that one be 21 years old to drink. In order to accommodate its patrons, many of whom were under the age limit, the bar stocked non-alcoholic beverages. However if someone ordered a hard drink, the bartender never asked for ID.

"A coke please," Adam nervously ordered as he looked around. Everyone seemed to be with someone, and he was disappointed. He reasoned that he couldn't be expected to make out the very first time. If he became a regular and a familiar face, he might meet some like-minded men. That thought helped relieve some of his stress, and he relaxed somewhat. He even got into a conversation with the bartender when the man had a short break.

Adam was faced away from the bar, observing the gyrating, dancing bodies. He could clearly see that some of the men were sporting erections and he got one himself so he turned back to the bar when he heard a voice behind him.

"Hi," the voice said. "I think I know you from school." Adam's heart skipped a beat. He turned around to see who had spoken. Yes, the guy did look familiar, but Adam could not quite place where he knew him from in the overcrowded University.

"Yeah," he said to the good looking older man facing him. "I know you from somewhere." Adam faced the man and tried to place him as he studied him. The guy was about 5'11" inches tall. He was dark and swarthy and drop dead gorgeous (Adam thought). His dark brown eyes were almost black and were quietly seducing Adam. It was clear that the man's body was muscular and mature. Adam was now feeling very inferior. He was 5'9" and very thin. He had blue eyes, sandy blonde hair and his ears protruded from his face, not helped by his buzz cut which was fashionable at the time.

"I know," the man said. "English Lit. You're in my English Lit class." He extended his hand and said. My name's Evan. There's an empty table over there. Why don't you bring your drink over there and we'll get better acquainted."

"Great," Adam said. "My name's Adam." He could hardly contain his excitement. He actually had made a possible friend in his first hour in a queer bar.

The table sat four and Adam expected Evan to sit across from him, but he sat down on Adam's right so that they both faced the dance floor. Adam continued to sip his coke, but Evan was drinking something much stronger.

"You're under twenty-one," Evan observed. "Would you like me to get you something stronger?"

"I tasted a whiskey sour once, at a graduation party. I kinda liked it, and it was pretty mild."

"I'll be right back," Evan said. He went to the bar and came back with a whiskey sour.

"What do I owe you?" Adam asked.

"It's on me," Evan said, "but if you insist on payment, I'll charge you a smile. I saw you when I came in and I haven't seen you smile yet. You look scared silly. First time, isn't it?"

"Yeah," Adam nodded shyly.

"Relax, babe," Evan said. "I won't bite, but I will admit that I am cruising you. I figure that you don't recognize the signs. Frankly, I think you're hot. Do you live on campus? I'm living there now, but when I find the right roommate, I want to get a place off campus next year, but I don't want a houseful of slobs. I'd like to be able to swing it with one roommate. Hey do you wanna dance?"

Adam couldn't believe how fast Evan talked and how many questions he asked without waiting for an answer. Adam had never danced with a man before, but he didn't mind the thought of being held in Evan's muscular arms.

"Yeah," he muttered grinning, "but I don't know how to follow."

"No need to follow or lead. Just put both your arms around my waist and I'll do the same."

On the dance floor, Evan pulled Adam tightly into him and made sure that their crotches were touching. Adam almost swooned when he felt Evan's hardness against him. He pushed even harder so that Evan could feel his erection also. He rested his head on Evan's shoulder and closed his eyes, letting Evan steer him smoothly across the dance floor. It felt so good, so right. He wished it could last all night, however the music stopped, and the two men stopped dancing. They continued to hold tightly to each other. They gazed longingly into each other's eyes and let their lips touch. Neither had taken the initiative. It just happened mutually between them.

"Are we going to make love tonight," Evan asked, "or are you against making love on the first date?"

"I didn't think we were on a date."

"Really? Well I did buy you a drink so that makes it an official date," Evan laughed.

"I'm a technical virgin," Adam informed Evan as they headed back to their table.

"What does that mean?" Evan wanted to know, so Adam told him about his seduction by a gentleman called Eve.

"It was my only time so I consider myself a technical virgin. I was too scared to really participate. I just went through the motions." Adam explained. "Tell me about your first time."

"It was during basic training. I got an overnight pass and my buddy and I went into the nearest town. I wasn't looking for any action and it didn't strike me at the time, but my buddy wasn't looking either. We ended up in a cheap hotel and he took my cherry. It was the greatest day of my life until then, and that's when I realized that sex with a man was what I really wanted. Now that the war is over, I want much more. I want someone to really love me and I want to love him back." Evan leaned over the table and kissed Adam on the lips. It was a mother/son kiss, but Adam kissed back harder.

"Are we starting something?" Evan asked in all innocence.

"I sure hope so," Adam replied.

"My roommate went home for the weekend. Let's dump this place and go back to my room," Evan pleaded.

"But I never answered if I would do it on a first date," Adam said and burst out laughing.

They left in a big hurry, and when they reached Evan's room, Adam said in alarm, "My room is a few doors down the hall. We'll have to be careful that nobody sees us." The hall was deserted and they rushed into Evan's room and locked the door.

CHAPTER TWO

When the two young men were alone in Evan's room, there was an awkward silence. Not really knowing how to proceed, Adam examined the room. Both beds were made up with hospital corners. The desks were full of books, but they were all neatly stacked. One of the desks had a portable typewriter placed in the center. There was an empty waste basket next to each desk. There was none of the usual dormitory clutter. In fact, there was no stench of dirty socks and underwear. Adam found out later that the laundry was placed in a ditty bag, and stowed in the closet.

"This place looks ready for a military inspection," Adam said incredulously.

"I keep it that way," Evan said. "Except for when I was in the field, we had to keep our barracks looking this way."

"You were in combat then?" Adam asked.

"Yes, ETO. But let's not talk about that. Let's talk about you. I can't believe that I never noticed how hot you are."

"I'm not hot at all," Adam said. "You're the hot one. Just look at your muscles." Adam reached out to squeeze Evan's arm, but Evan grabbed him, pulled the younger man to him and began to kiss him passionately.

After a while Evan pulled away and said, "Let's agree that we are both hot and hopefully very attracted to each other." Evan pulled Adam's sweater off him and started to undo the buttons on his shirt. Not knowing what else to do, Adam began to unbutton Evan's shirt. Like most men of that time, they both wore undershirts, and Evan pulled Adam's off and then removed his own. Now they were naked from the waist up.

Adam gasped. Evan had a scar running down the center of his chest from his breasts to his navel.

"I should have warned you," Evan said. "I was severely wounded in Normandy. I took several bullets in my chest, but luckily they all missed my heart and no major arteries were torn. The medics were able to patch me up until I was evacuated to a field hospital where the doctors saved my life. There's one bullet very close to my heart that they left in me."

"My God," was all Adam could say.

"Anyway I get a nice monthly pension from The Uncle along with my Purple Heart. That and the GI Bill are the only reasons I can afford this school."

"You're a regular hero," Adam said. "I feel like a real slacker."

"Nonsense!" Evan said. "But you do owe me for protecting your liberties. How would you like to make love to a soldier who fought for you?" As he asked this question, Evan removed his penny loafers and dropped his pants rapidly. He was not wearing underwear. Adam quickly followed.

Now they stood at the side of Evan's bed totally naked. They eyed each other up and down admiring what they saw. Finally Adam said, "You're beautiful." Not only was Evan as muscular as Adam had deemed him to be, he was beautifully hung. He had a good size scrotum, but his uncut cock was longer and hung below his balls. Adam wanted to reach out and grab Evan's cock, but he was frightened.

"Wow! You're an eyeful too, Babe. Look at that dick. You gotta be eight inches." Adam was fully erect and probably measured a little larger than that. Evan wasn't frightened like Adam. He reached out and began to caress Adam's cock. Adam began to purr like a kitten. Evan pulled him into bed with him.

The lovers lay in bed facing each other. Their cocks ground together, and Adam had to reach down to rearrange things a little because his cock was in a bad position. Evan put his hands on Adam's ass cheeks and pulled him tighter. "Adam, don't be put off by what I am about to say, but I gotta say it. I've fucked lots of guys in my life, but it didn't mean anything. Right now I feel like my life is fulfilled. You are what I have been waiting for. I think I love you. No, I know I love you. Do you believe in love at first sight?"

"I never thought about it, but it happens in the movies all the time. It's OK that I'm five years younger than you?" Adam asked.

"Yeah. I always wanted a twinkie."

Adam laughed. "Actually, I think I'm too old to be a twinkie."

"Whatever."

Evan climbed on top of Adam and started to kiss him. Underneath their joined bodies, he was caressing Adam's cock. Little by little he worked his way down Adam's body, kissing his ears, his nipples, his belly button and finally his balls. When Adam's squirming reached a peak, Evan wrapped his hand around Adam's cock and took as much as he could into his mouth. His tongue licked Adam's shaft and his lips sucked and pumped as they rode up and down the length of Adam's cock. All the while his free hand was tickling and caressing Adam's balls.

"I'm cumming, Ev," Adam yelled. Evan had no intention of stopping and Adam began to squirt generously into Evan's mouth as he emitted a banshee wail. Evan held Adam's cock in his mouth until he felt it softening. Only then did he release his younger lover and crawl back up to lie beside him. Adam leaned over and began to kiss Evan,

"Guess what? I think I love you too," Adam said. "Now just tell me if you want me to suck you off or if you want to fuck me. I'll do whatever you want me to do.

"Suck me, honey. We'll fuck each other in the morning."

The following morning was Saturday. They woke up clinging to each other. "I've got to get to my room and grab a towel and my toothbrush," Adam said. "Boy, I really have to pee." He jumped out of bed and dressed rapidly. He opened the door. Nobody was in the hall, probably due to the early hour. Adam ran to the bathroom to relieve himself. As he left, Evan came in. He put his military toiletry kit on a chair and took the same urinal Adam had just vacated. Adam patted him on the rump. "I'll be right back," he said. "After we shower, we can continue what we started last night."

"Yes sir, Captain," Evan quipped back.

They were alone in the four stall shower, but they refrained from touching. However, they kept looking longingly at each other and mouthing the words, "I love you!" They did what they always did in the morning. They shit, showered and shaved. Then they returned to their respective rooms. Adam's roommate was snoring away. Even though he knew that in a few minutes he would be naked, Adam dressed fully. He was about to leave when he heard his roommate stir.

"Hey what time did you get in, stud? I got home at one and you weren't here yet."

"I probably got in a little later than that. Listen, I'll be out all day today and tomorrow. I'll see you tomorrow night."

"She must be one hot chick," Marty said. He rolled over and fell asleep again.

Seconds later, Adam was back in Evan's room. He locked the door behind him. Evan was lying naked in his bed. He beckoned to Adam and pointed to his nightstand. There was an open jar of Vaseline on the stand. As soon as Evan was satisfied that Adam had seen the Vaseline, he rolled over on his back and put a pillow under his buttocks. He spread his legs and said, "Grease me up good, buddy. This is our honeymoon."

Adam took a generous amount of the grease and shoved it gently up Evan's ass. He rubbed it in good as Evan moaned with pleasure. Then he greased his stiff cock and stood between Evan's legs. He lined himself up and placed his cock head on Evan's love hole.

"Don't be afraid to go right in, babe," Evan said. "It's a well stretched canal." He wasn't kidding. Adam slipped in almost too easily, and he wasn't small either." After Adam entered Evan he did nothing. He wanted to savor the warm moist feeling.

"Gawd," he said. "This is even better than a blow job. I'm so glad I'm queer. No woman would let me do this."

"Fuck me," Evan ordered. "I want you to gush inside of me."

"I won't disobey such a delicious order," Adam said, as he started to stroke. On the in stroke Evan contracted the muscles in his anus, and he released them on the out stroke. Adam was going crazy and came way too fast. Well, maybe not too fast for an 18 year old. His body collapsed on Evan's and they began to kiss madly. Whenever they came up for air they whispered to each other *I love you.*

After they recovered, Adam said, "Fuck me now baby, but remember I'm a virgin, or at least, my ass is virtually a virgin."

"Lie on your stomach, honey," Evan said. Adam rolled over and soon felt the cold Vaseline going up his ass. Evan inserted one finger and began to ream Adam's ass, trying to stretch it. When Adam was comfortable and enjoying the ass massage, Evan added a second finger and reamed some more. After the third finger was added and Adam's ass was well reamed, Evan removed the three fingers. He inserted his cock up to Adam's sphincter. Adam winced, but Evan proceeded to enter him slowly. Adam was in great pain. When Evan was all the way in, he lay perfectly still.

Evan could tell when Adam was relaxed. "Are you all right?" he asked.

"Yes Ev, the pain is going away. You can fuck me now."

Evan was glad to do as instructed. He fucked Adam doggie style, but he also instructed Adam on how to contract his ass muscles. Adam learned quickly, and pushed Evan over the top. When Adam felt Evan's juices inside of him, he began to cry tears of joy.

"What's the matter, sweet?" Evan asked.

"Nothing. I'm just so damned happy."

They stayed in bed, hugging, cuddling and fondling each other for some time until finally Adam said. "I think I'm hungry. Let's go eat off campus. I don't want my roommate to see me. I told him I would be gone until tomorrow night."

They dressed reluctantly. It was a tedious job. They kept grabbing at each other and pulling off articles of clothing as soon as they were donned. Their game was accompanied by lots of giggling, like two young school girls. They weren't even aware of how silly they were being. Adam left the room first. He looked up and down the hall cautiously until it was safe to leave. He waited at the front entrance until Evan joined him a few moments later.

Just as they met, another student entered the dorm. Evan put on an act. "Hi Adam. Long time no see. How are you doing?"

By now the student was gone and Adam began to laugh. "Come on. Let's get out of here. I'm starving."

After that weekend, they made love at every opportunity, but opportunities were rare. They even paid for a room at the YMCA a couple of times. Adam had always thought of the YMCA as being a very religious organization and the facility as a retreat of some kind. He was shocked at how much overt action was going on between the guests. Evan also introduced him to the baths where they could rent a private room for the night. They were often approached by other men who wanted to join them. They always said no, except for one time.

Evan recognized a scared little virgin when he saw one. The boy said that he was nineteen, but Evan put him at seventeen, maybe even sixteen. They took the boy (never got his name) to their room and broke him in properly. He left about 1 AM thanking Adam and Evan profusely for making his dreams come true.

At the end of the first semester, Evan's roommate announced that he was transferring to UCSD. He had been in San Diego when he was in the navy and decided that he really wanted to move there after the war. Evan ran to the Housing Office even before his *roomie* made the announcement, and he arranged for Adam to transfer in with him. From the time Adam moved in with Evan, they were together almost every night until the night Evan passed away.

There were some minor exceptions, of course, like business trips, and family times before they came out, and each had to attend these events alone. The first break of the spring semester came at Easter. The men spent the school break with their respective families. They had not yet determined how and when to come out, or if they ever would. In the future if they were ever questioned as to why two grown men were living together they would say that they were half-brothers. They would say that their mother had remarried after Evan's father died.

The story that they were brothers became more believable as time progressed. From the time they met, Adam began to work out with Evan. Adam grew another inch, and his skinny body began to fill out until he was a bulky hunk. Evan kidded him that he was like an ad for Charles Atlas. The bottom line was that they were both buff and looked more like brothers, in spite of the fact that Evan was so dark and Adam was so fair.

More important than Adam's physical transformation was the fact that with each day they grew more and more in love. When class schedules parted them even for a few short hours, they felt as if a part of their body had been removed. They skipped meals often, because they would hold so tight to one another, that they couldn't let go in order to get to the dining hall. They weren't even having sex. When they did have sex, it was always like the first time. Fireworks exploded as they both had amazing orgasms.

By the time they were juniors it was becoming more and more obvious that it was getting impossible to hide their feelings from their families. They wanted desperately to announce their union, come what may. In those days being homosexual was tantamount to a career death unless you were a dress designer or a hair stylist. Adam's biggest fear was being disowned by his parents, and he desperately wanted to graduate from college. He had no GI Bill to help him like Evan did.

They discussed what course of action to take and finally decided that they would keep their secret until after graduation. Then they would both seek employment as far from New York as possible, and they would move to the city where the first one of them gained employment. It might be possible never to come out to their parents

Once they had made a firm decision as to their future plans, they relaxed quite a bit. Their love making became more daring, adventuresome and more than a little kinky. They discovered that they both loved rimming a clean pink ass. They found a little footstool in a second hand furniture store and cut a hole in the middle. One of them would lie on his back on the floor. The other would place the stool over his partner's face and then sit on it. His ass would protrude invitingly right onto his partner's face and the rimming would begin and sometimes last for hours. Adam smiled in his sleep remembering the ever ready footstool.

There was a quiet knock on Adam's apartment door, which did not stir him from his reveries. The knocking got louder and more insistent. Finally Adam was brought back to reality and he was in his little apartment in The Sunnydale House. He rushed to answer the door, this time forgetting his nudity.

"Hey man," Jamie said, rushing in and closing the door. "You don't want those horny old ladies out there to see that massive schlong of yours, now do you?"

Adam turned red as a beet, and quickly grabbed his robe. "I'm really sorry Jamie," he said. I always sleep nude and I forgot myself."

"It's dinner time," Jamie reminded Adam. Do you want to pick me up or should I wait for you while you dress?"

"Please wait," Adam said. "I'll just be a moment." He went into the bathroom and washed the sleep from his eyes. The clothes he had worn earlier in the day were still on a boudoir chair in his bedroom, and he slipped into them in record time.

"See," he announced, "I'm ready." Jamie crooked his arm and Adam put his arm through Jamie's as they left the room and started to walk to the dining room. Jamie found them a table for two in a quiet corner. After they were comfortably seated and had placed their orders, Jamie asked, "How did you and Evan meet? I don't think you ever told me. I'd like to know, if it isn't too painful for you."

"Talking about Evan can never be too painful. We met at the beginning of our college careers. We were both majoring in business administration. As lower freshman, our rooms were a few doors apart. We managed to get a room together for our upper freshman year. After that, we rented a studio apartment in Greenwich Village. Those were heavenly days. We worked hard and life was like an extended honeymoon. We were too much in love to realize how hard our lives would be living as a gay couple, especially at work, where we were very closeted. Things are much better these days for the young people. There are plenty of bigots still around, but for the most part, people have become more understanding and tolerant."

The waitress interrupted Adam's narrative. She served their fruit cocktail appetizers and asked if she could get them anything else. Jamie smiled and said that they were just fine.

"In our senior year we began to apply for jobs in distant cities. Evan's age and experience may have been influential in his getting a job before me. He was interviewed in New York for an up and coming electronics firm located in Miami. We had no idea at the time what a great field electronics would turn out to be. I lied to my family and told them that I had landed a job in Miami and was moving down there. My mother wept and carried on. I had to remind her that I wasn't going off to war, and I was only a phone call away. Evan bought an old pre-war jalopy and we drove down to Miami with only our clothes. We didn't want to spend money on hotels so we spelled each other driving and drove straight through. In Miami we stayed in a motel for a week or so until we were able to rent a furnished apartment. I have to tell you that without Evan's pension we couldn't have made it."

The waitress came by to pick up their empty fruit dishes. "Your steaks will be ready in a few minutes," she said, smiling as she left the table.

"In those days," Adam continued, "air conditioning was sparse, and Miami had a reputation of being a place you went to on the way to the cemetery. There weren't a lot of young folks rushing to settle here. I had no trouble getting a job as office manager/ controller for a growing legal firm. They specialized in immigration law. A few years later, when the Cubans started to come in droves, I ended up with a staff of twenty people. Half of them were bilingual and I studied Spanish in night school myself."

"In the meantime, Evan's firm landed a small contract to manufacture computer microchips. When I say, a small contract, I don't exaggerate. Most people had no idea what a computer was at that time. Needless to say, it didn't take many more years and the firm was swamped with microchip orders. Financially, we were both doing well. I feel sorry for young men and women today. There are no more ground floors to get in on."

The waitress came by with their steaks. Adam hadn't realized how hungry he was, and he stopped talking while they ate their entrees and the ice cream they ordered for dessert. After dinner, Adam asked Jamie to forgive him, but he wanted to go to bed. He was so tired.

"I can find my own way," Adam said. "Don't worry about me." Jamie gave Adam a manly hug and then went to the card room to see if he could get into a game.

Adam returned to his apartment and stripped. He usually showered in the morning, but he felt achy all over and decided to take a nice hot bath. He filled the tub with the hottest water the taps would yield. It was a little too hot to get into so he let some water out and added some cold water. Now it was perfect.

He settled down in the tub and slouched until the water line was at his neck. It felt so good. He closed his eyes and his thoughts took him back to a happier time.

————————

He and Evan had just purchased their first home. They avoided the growing congestion in Miami and found a beautiful three bedroom home with a swimming pool in Hollywood, Florida. They both had a bit of a commute, but gas was cheap in those days and the highways were not congested. They each had new cars provided by their companies as an added perk. Life was treating them well.

They had worked hard all day, opening cartons and stowing their worldly goods neatly into places where it all belonged. "Let's take a bath and soak our aching muscles," Evan suggested. They drew the bath and got in facing each other. Evan's big toe began to play with Adam's cock so Adam did the same to Evan.

"I've got an idea," Evan said. He crawled up the tub until his buttocks was situated over Adam's cock. He lowered himself slowly until Adam's cock began to slip into Evan's ass.

"I knew we wouldn't need lubricant in the water," Evan said. He began to bob up and down. The kinkiness of the situation turned Adam on and he came quickly.

"Let me try that now," Adam said and they switched positions. That night they slept well and happily in their new home.

The next morning, they had coffee and an English muffin for breakfast. They left the house together to go their separate ways. When they closed the front door, they both froze in their tracks. Painted in red across the white front door was the following warning.

FAGGOTS GO AWAY
OR ELSE

CHAPTER THREE

The first thing they did was to go back into the house and call the police. The police came out and took pictures of the front door, but admitted honestly that there was little they could do. They promised to patrol the street and keep an eye on the house. In the meantime, the presence of the police cars attracted all the neighbors, who got a good look at the front door. Well, there was no need to pretend to be half-brothers anymore. They were definitely out of the lavender closet. If this hate crime had happened today it would have been plastered all over the newspaper. Fortunately for Adam and Evan the event remained on their street.

They were too shook up to go to work and so they called in sick. They couldn't explain the real reason they couldn't come in, because at work they were in the closet. Evan went out and bought a can of paint. They repainted the door and spent most of the day unpacking the rest of the boxes and getting everything put in place.

By mid afternoon, it looked like they had been there forever. Figuring that it was safe to leave the house in broad daylight, they took a trip to the supermarket and stocked the fridge and the pantry.

About 5 PM there was a knock at the door. A good looking, young couple stood at the door with a towhead little boy clutching his daddy's knee. The woman held a covered tray and the man stuck his hand out. "Hi," he said. "We live next door, on your right, and we want you to know that the filth you found on your door does not represent the sentiments of the neighborhood. We're here to welcome you."

Adam was speechless, but Evan said, "Please come in and sit down."

Evan took them into the living room. "I'm Evan and this is my partner Adam." (There, he said it.)

"We're Jack and Ellie Bingham, and this little rascal who won't let go of my knee is Billy. Say 'hello' Billy." Billy was mute.

"Here's a batch of cookies I whipped up for the occasion," Ellie said.

Evan took the covered tray and asked, "Can I get you something to drink and we can have some cookies with it?"

"Not tonight," Ellie said, "but I want you to know that we have a block party on the last Sunday evening of every month, weather permitting, and it usually does. It's bring your own food and drink. We block traffic off at both ends of the street, and set up bridge tables at the north corner. It gets going about 4:30 so you guys be sure to be there."

Little Billy found his voice. "Can I have a cookie?" he asked politely. Adam looked at Ellie who nodded. He uncovered the tray which was full of chocolate chip cookies, and held it out to Billy. "Thank you, sir," the little boy said politely.

The adults made small talk for a little while and filled themselves in on their work, how long they had lived in Florida (nobody was a native) and where they had come from. When the Bingham's got up to leave, little Billy said, "I like them Mommy. They're nice." Everyone laughed. Just as they started down the front walk another couple came up the walk. The woman was carrying a casserole dish. They appeared to be in their late thirties, somewhat older than the Binghams. The two couples chatted for a minute. The lady with the casserole leaned down and kissed Billy on his head as the Bingham's left. Adam and Evan waited for the new comers at the front door.

"Hello," the man said to them. "I'm Ben Richter and this is my wife Sarah. We want to welcome you to the neighborhood. We live next door on your left." Ben spoke with a heavy German accent.

"Please come in," Adam said. He was beginning to feel much better. "I'm Adam and my partner's name is Evan." He was proud of himself when he said 'my partner.'

"I've got a tuna casserole here for you two boys. I hope you like tuna," Sarah said.

"We love it," Evan said. "Thank you so much. I'll put it in the fridge and be back in a minute." Adam took the Richters into the living room and motioned for them to be seated. Evan returned and sat down.

Ben started the conversation. "About that garbage on your front door," he said and rolled his eyes, "you find hatred all over the world. At least you could remove the hate, but we can never remove these." Ben held out his arm and turned it palm up. He was wearing a short sleeve shirt, and Adam and Evan could clearly see some numbers tattooed in blue on his forearm. "We survived the camps. We survived the holocaust," he said.

"My God," Adam said.

"Were you both in the service during the war?" Ben asked.

"I was too young, but Evan was nearly killed in the war," Adam informed them.

"Then we owe you our lives," Ben said. "I will be forever in your debt for having liberated us."

"You owe us nothing," Evan said. "We fought for our own liberties as well."

"I want to tell you a story," Ben said. "There were homosexuals in our camp along with us Jews. One night a young boy, no more than sixteen, came into our barracks. He was a young homosexual, a Christian boy. He was crying and he begged us to harbor him as a Jew. The homosexuals were treated worse than we were, and to make matters worse, although the German soldiers pretended to despise them, young Hans told us that he was raped by them almost every night. We had extra yellow armbands from dead comrades and we substituted one of them for his pink one. When Hans came to us, the war was winding down. One day we woke and found the camp deserted. The Germans had all fled during the night. I rushed to the women's barracks and found Sarah still alive. She was very weak. The Germans had experimented on her and we will never have children. Sarah, Hans and I had managed to survive. All we needed to do was to wait for the Americans to arrive. I had relatives in Miami, who brought us here. We pretended that Hans was my little brother and got him here too."

"Where is Hans?" Adam asked. There were tears in his eyes.

"He's well." Ben said. "He and his partner live and work in Ft Lauderdale. Barry is all American. He was born in Detroit," Ben announced proudly. "Friday night they will come for Sabbath dinner. Would you also honor us with your presence and you can meet Hans and Barry."

Evan and Adam looked at each other. Evan said, "It will be our honor, and I can't wait to meet your kid brothers."

Ben and Sophie got up to leave. Ben put one arm on Adam's shoulder and the other on Evan's. "You and we," he said, "we must always be vigilant. We can't allow hate to prevail here in America like it infested Germany."

When they were gone, Adam began to cry and Evan took him in his arms. "I'm OK," Adam said. "Whoever those bastards are, the whole neighborhood is against them. I'm very happy we moved to this street, Evan. I was thinking that we could gauge everyone's reaction to meeting us at the block party next week. We might even figure out who painted our door. Maybe we can urge Hans and Barry to come to the party."

Bright sunlight poured into Adam's bedroom waking him up. It was 6:45 AM on the day before Evan's funeral. Evan's funeral! Adam still couldn't believe that Evan had left him. It was too much for him to bear. He busied himself by getting ready for the day. In less than an hour he would meet Jamie for breakfast.

He felt so all alone. His dear friends, Hans Richter and Barry Stern, had passed away a decade ago. Barry went first. Hans followed him by just a few months. Adam was certain that Hans could not survive this life without Barry. He knew it was wrong, but he wished for the same fate as Hans, and quickly.

At breakfast Jamie asked him if he would like to do anything today. "Do you need to shop or anything?"

"No, my dear boy. You have taken care of everything." Jamie had arranged for food to be served in the dining room after the funeral. Outside of The Sunnydale House residents, Adam did not expect more than a few acquaintances. Most of his and Evan's friends were dead. Adam was a sole survivor.

After breakfast Adam excused himself from Jamie, and found a seat on the front veranda. The sun felt good on his old bones. He turned his face to greet the warming orb, and he thought he heard laughter. Yes, he clearly heard Hans and Barry laughing. Then Ben and Sarah joined in. Finally he could hear Evan's distinctive laugh louder than all the rest. They were all having such a good time.

———————————

It was the first Friday night in their new home. Adam and Evan were walking across their front lawn to the Richters. Adam carried Sarah's empty casserole dish and Evan carried a bottle of red wine. There was a strange car in the Richter's driveway. "I guess the young queers are here already," Evan said jokingly.

"Please Evan. You know how I hate that word."

"I would never use derogatory words in public. It was just a joke between us girls."

"You are incorrigible! I don't know why I put up with you," Adam said.

"You put up with me because you love me."

"Yeah, I guess that's the reason," Adam smiled at Evan.

They rang the doorbell and the door was opened by a drop dead gorgeous young man about Adam's age. He was nearly six feet tall. His eyes were blue and his hair was platinum blond. He was smiling broadly and he could dazzle you with that smile.

"Adam and Evan?" he asked quizzically. He had no trace of an accent and Evan wondered if he might not be Barry, and that maybe he had jumped to a stereotypical conclusion.

"I'm Hans," the young man said and held out his hand, "I am always so pleased to meet a liberator. Please come in."

"You people are going to embarrass me to death," Evan said. "I did nothing more than my duty."

Hans introduced them to Barry, who did not hold out his hand at all. Instead he gave each of them a good strong hug. He said something similar to what Hans had said, but completely different. "I'm always glad to meet a brother who isn't ashamed to be what he is, and let people know it."

Adam and Evan felt a great pang of guilt. They had intended to pass themselves off as brothers, but were accidently outed by the hate patrol. Ironically, they looked no more like brothers than Hans and Ben.

During the evening Hans and Barry did most of the talking. They were exuberant about their jobs, their lives and most of all their love for each other. They were not embarrassed to show Ben and Sarah how much they loved them also. The best part was that they talked openly about their homosexual lifestyle.

"There's a section of Ft. Lauderdale where more and more gays are moving in," Barry said. This was the first time Evan and Adam had heard the word 'gay.' "It's becoming a little Mecca. The best part is that a couple of gay bars have opened up. It's great because we can hang out there with our buddies. We're having dinner at one of the bars tomorrow. Why don't you guys join us?"

"You should go," Ben said. "Sarah and I had dinner there with the boys a couple of weeks ago. The food was wonderful and also I found out that these two have a lot of nice friends. I would urge you to go and I would love it if you would all become friends."

"Enough talk," Sarah said. "Dinner is ready. Come to the dining room."

"Have you ever had a traditional Jewish Sabbath dinner?" Hans asked. Evan and Adam shook their heads. "You'll love it," Hans continued. Your taste buds will salivate, but you better have plenty of alka seltzer at home. I had to wait until we got to the States to savor it, but boy, it was worth the wait."

"Jewish cuisine was the final step in converting Hans to Judaism," Barry said. "It was the food that did it." That brought much laughter to the table.

"My conversion isn't kosher however," Hans said. "Barry wouldn't let me get circumcised at my age. I wanted to do it, but he said absolutely no, so when the rabbi asked, I said I was cut. I prayed and prayed that he wouldn't want to look for himself. But I did study, and I had a Bar Mitzvah last year. I wish you guys were here so you could have been at the party. We had a blast."

The food was as delicious as Hans had promised and Evan and Adam were introduced to a couple of new dishes like matzoh ball soup and chopped liver spread. Hans and Barry kept everyone in stitches telling tales about some of their friends, straight and gay. The evening was almost nonstop laughter.

During dinner, Barry and Hans kept leaning over and kissing each other and holding hands, right in front of Ben and Sarah. Adam and Evan had trained themselves not to show any affection in public and they really didn't know how to react to this public display of male to male affection. All of a sudden, out of the blue, in the middle of a laugh, Hans asked, "Evan, do you love Adam? Adam, do you love Evan?"

They both looked at Ben and Sarah thoroughly embarrassed. "Of course we do," Evan sputtered.

"You sure don't show it, man," Barry said. "Kiss each other for God's sake."

"Yeah," Ben said. "Kiss each other." Ben, Sarah, Barry and Hans began tapping on their wine glasses as if they were at a wedding trying to urge the bride and groom to kiss. Red faced, Evan leaned into Adam and kissed him lightly on the lips.

"You call that a kiss?" Hans said. "You do it like this." He leaned into Barry. Their mouths parted and they began to soul kiss. The kiss went on and on.

Finally Ben said, "Enough already. You two are embarrassing me. Your old bedroom is upstairs, Hans. Go you two, before it's too late." Everyone laughed so hard their sides hurt.

———————

Sitting on the veranda at The Sunnydale House, Adam could still hear the laughter. The laughter reverberated in his ears until he could feel a headache coming on. Then he realized that tomorrow was Evan's funeral. The headache got worse as he buried his head in his hands and wept and wept and wept. Suddenly the semi-tropical sun was too much for Adam to bear. He went upstairs to his apartment and closed the door. He dialed Jamie's telephone number even though he knew that Jamie wasn't in his apartment. Leaving a message on Jamie's answering machine, he politely asked Jamie not to pick him up for lunch. He said that he wasn't hungry but that he would meet him for dinner.

He stripped as he always did before getting into bed. It was warm in the room and he lay down on top of the covers. He could hear birds chirping outside his window, but everything got really silent as he slipped into a fretful sleep.

———————

He and Evan were standing on the front porch of Hans and Barry's house. They knocked on the door and Barry let them in. As soon as they were inside, they were literally attacked by the homeowners who covered them with kisses and hugged them tightly. There was no question that Hans and Barry were very demonstrative and very kissy, kissy. Adam and Evan were just the opposite. They had made a career out of being in the closet, and covering up there sexual identity. Hans and Barry made them feel guilty.

Barry opened four beer bottles and handed one to each of them. "It's a little early yet," he said. "Our reservation is for 7:30 and we can walk over in five minutes, so drink up me hearties."

"How did you two meet?" Evan asked them.

They both broke out laughing. Did these two ever stop laughing?

"I'll tell." Hans said. "I had a blind date with some guy whose name I can't remember. A few days before the date he called to ask me if I would mind if we double dated. He said that blind dates could sometimes be awkward and this way if things started to go south, there would be another couple there to relieve the pressure. So my date asked a friend of his to double date with us. Well, as luck would have it, the friend also had a blind date for that night, so a double date suited him just fine also."

Barry picked up the story and continued. "I was the other guy's blind date. To make a long story short, neither of us liked our dates, but we sure liked each other. We never even said anything to each other. We just seemed to read one another's minds."

"Yeah," Hans said. "Halfway through dinner I got up to pee and Barry said he needed to go also. We slipped out the back door and took off, leaving those poor guys with four meals to pay for."

Barry and Hans burst into more laughter. Adam had to wonder how Hans could laugh so much after what he had been through. As if he could read his mind, Hans said, "You know, my life was hell until I somehow got the courage to hide in Ben's barracks. Now I am the luckiest guy in the world. I worshipped Jesus once. I still do. But he was never my Messiah. Ben and Sarah are my true Messiahs." Then he smiled at Barry. "Barry is a Messiah too, but in a much different way." He leaned into Barry and they began to kiss passionately.

It got a little too hot so Evan said, "If you two want to go to bed we can go to dinner alone."

"Not on your life," Hans said. "I am going to personally teach you two to enjoy life and love each other more." This statement coming from a holocaust survivor fueled Adam's guilt.

"I don't think I could love Evan more." Adam said.

"Never say never," Barry advised. "You'll see."

During dinner practically everyone in the restaurant came over to greet Barry and Hans. Did these two know everyone in the gay community? Apparently! They introduced Adam and Evan to everyone and the general sentiment was that Adam and Evan should hang out here more often so that they could all become better friends.

"You *should* come here more often," Hans said. "After dinner we'll hang out at the piano and sing. You guys must learn to let your hair down, and have some fun. I get the feeling that your up tightness comes from hiding who you are from the world. Believe me you have nothing to prove. If you are vital links at work, it won't make any difference to your bosses."

Adam had his doubts about that and Evan was in full agreement. They had a wonderful time with their new friends and hated when it was time to drive home. In the car Evan said that he could not believe that Hans was so upbeat after having been continually raped by German soldiers and having survived the holocaust. They agreed that he was an amazing man.

In bed that night as they were cuddling, Adam asked Evan, "How do you think they would take it at work if you came out?"

"I really don't know, but I'd probably get fired. What about you?"

"Pretty much the same thing. I think I need to get laid," Adam said, and cuddled closer.

Adam pushed his erection against Evan's thigh. Their lips met in a passionate embrace. Their hands groped and found each other's cocks and each began to stroke the other.

"Suck my cock, please," Evan pleaded and Adam gladly obliged. They assumed their favorite fallatio position. Evan lay on his back and Adam got on his knees between Evan's legs. In this position Adam's tongue could slide up and down the underside of Evan's shaft. They both found the underside of the shaft more erogenous than the head or even the balls. Only the entrance to their asses was more erogenous than that. Adam began to stroke Evan's cock with his tongue and his fingers, just as the phone rang.

"Shit," Evan said as he reached for the phone. Adam kept on sucking.

"Hi, this is Hans," a cheery voice said. "I'm just calling to make sure that you two are making love and going all out. I hope there are no hang ups in your bedroom."

Evan started to laugh. "I assure you that we go all out in private. We don't hold back. It's just that showing affection in public is something we are going to have to learn."

"Good, because I'm not going to give up my role as mentor. I intend to get you two to stop worrying and enjoy life. Just take into account how good we've got it, compared to life in a concentration camp. We are all so blessed," Hans said wistfully.

"You're right, dear friend," Evan said. "Now will you please hang up so Adam can resume sucking my cock?" They could both hear Hans laughing hysterically as he hung up the phone.

CHAPTER FOUR

The phone rang again. It took Adam a moment to realize it was not ringing in his dream, but in his room in the present. He picked it up.

"Adam, it's Jamie. You're sleeping too much. It's almost dinner time. Get yourself ready and I'll be by in a half hour."

"Yes, of course. You're right. I'll be ready when you get here."

Adam got through dinner like a robot. He had no appetite, but he ate everything. Everything was delicious but he tasted nothing. He went back to his apartment right after dinner and Jamie didn't argue with him. He figured he would battle Adam's retreat into another world after the funeral.

Adam wondered if he could fall asleep after having slept most of the day so he took a Tylenol PM to help him along.

_____

"Hey wake up, sleepy head," Evan said while shaking Adam's shoulder. "We need a break from long hours of studying. There's a drag show at The Male Room tonight. Let's go."

They were studying for final exams in their senior year. Adam was exhausted and had fallen asleep. "We shouldn't waste the time," he told Evan.

"I don't think my brain can absorb one more thing," Evan said, "so let's take that break."

"You win, big boy," Adam said. Adam still called Evan 'big boy' even though he had grown almost as tall and muscular as his partner during their college years.

The Male Room was very crowded. There were no tables available so they stood at the bar with many other guys. Each of them nursed a coke to legitimize their attendance. When they had come in this evening Adam spotted a sign in the lobby announcing that tonight's female impersonator would be "Mother Eve."

Six years had passed since Adam had been initiated into the homosexual world by Eve. He considered this a good omen for the upcoming exams. After about an hour, the dance floor was cleared off and an MC announced the dulcet rhythms of Mother Eve. Eve did not limit herself to the dance floor, but moved freely among the patrons while she sang. At one point she went right by Adam and Evan. She hesitated in front of Adam and finished her song facing him. The song was lewd and suggestive, and as she sang she wrapped her hand around Adam's crotch. Adam pulled back and Eve whispered in his ear. "Please wait for me after the show Adam. I'll come out in men's clothing and I really want to talk to you."

"What was that all about?" Evan asked.

"Honestly I have no idea, but she knew my name. It must be someone I know, but that I didn't know did drag." They waited about twenty minutes and then a very handsome gentleman about Evan's age approached them. Adam recognized Eve immediately. It was his Eve, his first time Eve. He was ecstatic, and gave Eve a big hug.

"How in the world did you ever recognize me?" Adam asked. "It's been a hundred years."

"You made a deep impression on me. After you left, I wanted to kick myself for not taking your telephone number and setting up another date. You were delicious you know."

"That's funny because I felt the same way. I so wanted a repeat performance. I waited more than two years for another go at it, with Evan here." Adam turned to Evan, took his hand and said, "Eve I'd like you to meet my partner, Evan."

The two men shook hands and Evan said, "It's kind of hard to call a handsome guy like you Eve. What's your real name?"

"It's Evan," Eve said, and broke out laughing. "Hey guys, if you have a half hour more, please hang out here. My partner is coming to pick me up. I'd like you to meet him. I'll buy you both a drink while you wait."

"Deal!" Evan said. "We weren't planning a quick exit."

Adam spotted an empty table and the three took seats there. Eve then returned to the bar and picked up fresh drinks for them. When she was seated, she proposed a toast and then Adam said, "You have no idea how scared I was when you picked me up on the subway."

"Not so. I could see you shaking in your boots, but the minute I went down on you, you became an animal. Is he still an animal, Evan?" Eve asked.

Evan laughed and nodded his head. "Thank God," he said. They all laughed.

Suddenly everything got black and Adam clearly heard a clock ticking. The sleeping pill had not lasted through the night. Adam looked at the luminous dial on his clock radio. It was 2:22 in the morning.

"Three twos," Adam thought. He tried to assign some significance to it, but nothing came to mind. Then it hit him like a thunderbolt. Before they ever met, Hans had gone to a plastic surgeon to have the numbers removed from his forearm. Ben and Sarah refused to do that. It was a constant reminder to everyone they met of the atrocities that man had committed against man. Hans told Adam once that the numbers on his forearm had been 22222, all twos.

"Hans," Adam called out in the night. "Are you here?"

There was silence in the room. Nevertheless Adam felt a presence surrounding him. He was not frightened. Whatever he was feeling was warm and comforting. He was certain that Hans was here with him and he felt much better. In fact, he fell asleep again.

It was the night of their first block party. Hans and Barry had promised to come. Adam and Evan were waiting at the Richter's for them to arrive. Adam had placed their neatly packed picnic basket on the floor beside his chair.

As if he was privy to all their conversations, Ben said, "We will watch carefully all the people tonight. If the bigots live on this street, they will give themselves away and I will know who they are. Barry and Hans will observe also. Hans will know."

Hans and Barry arrived shortly after that and they all went directly to the party. "Put your stuff here," a young voice yelled. It was Billy Bingham and he was pointing to one of the tables. Sarah scooped him up and started smothering him with kisses. Billy tried desperately to evade her clutches but she held him too tightly.

Barry and Hans were well known to the residents of the street, but everyone came over to meet the newcomers. Because they all seemed so friendly, Adam and Evan let their guards down, but Ben and Hans were observing closely. Finally Hans looked at Ben and he nodded. They had identified the culprits. The two of them then sat down smugly and enjoyed the rest of the evening.

Later that evening when everything was cleaned away, and Adam and Evan had returned home, there was a knock on their door. Adam went to open it and there stood Hans, Barry and Ben. They rushed in without invitation.

"We're pretty sure we know who the bigots may be, but we have to do some research. It may take a little while but we'll get back to you," Hans said.

———————

Adam had set his alarm clock to go off early on the morning of Evan's funeral and now it was ringing shrilly. He shut it off and crept wearily out of bed. As if nothing had happened; as if this was just another ordinary day; he went through his morning routines. After he showered and dressed in his only good suit, an all-purpose navy blue, he found a tie in his closet. He practically never wore a tie anymore. Without regard for a good match or not, he put it on, barely remembering how to tie a Windsor knot.

He almost always wore crew socks and sneakers these days, but he put on a pair of black knee high socks and his only pair of dress shoes. He looked in the mirror and supposed that he was ready for Evan's big send off. Then he sat down in a chair to wait for Jamie.

He rarely saw Jamie in a suit and was amazed at how handsome he looked. Neither of them felt like eating breakfast, but agreed to go to the dining room for a cup of coffee. The dining room was rather crowded with residents obviously dressed for a funeral. Steve Baron, the Executive Director, had reluctantly agreed to provide a bus to the funeral home, the cemetery, and then back to Sunnydale for the celebration of Evan's life, which Jamie had arranged for. As for Adam and Jamie they felt it more appropriate to go alone in a private vehicle. The funeral home was providing a limo for Adam and Jamie to go to the cemetery and back.

Adam sat with Jamie in the family receiving room before the service. After signing the guest book in the lobby, most of the attendees came into the room to express their condolences. During this ritual, which was distressing Adam no end, he suddenly regretted that he and Evan had not wished to adopt children like some of their friends had. It would have been nice to have some family around him to comfort him. Adam shook everyone's hand without really knowing who he was speaking to. He went through the entire funeral in a trance. He didn't wake up from it until he was back in Sunnydale at the reception.

———————

He and Evan were in The Star of David Funeral Home. They sat quietly in the second row, holding hands. In front of them sat Barry, Hans and Ben. Sarah had passed much too young at the age of fifty-five. The experiments the Nazis had performed on her in the camp had left her body permanently weakened. The Nazis had won after all. She got sick often and didn't seem to have enough of an immune system to ward off, and then fight off, these infections. She finally succumbed after a long bout with pneumonia. Barry and

Hans sat on each side of Ben. Each of them had an arm around him. Next to Adam sat the Binghams. Billy had flown down from FSU in Tallahassee to attend the funeral. Adam kept staring at him. He had grown into a handsome, athletic young man. Adam could not help thinking that some pretty young girl was going to be lucky enough someday to snare him.

After the funeral, everyone went back to Ben's house. Hans and Barry had provided delicious food for the mourners. A friend of theirs was a caterer and he had everything set up for them by the time everyone returned from the cemetery. He had also provided food for the people who would visit in the next three days to express condolences. Hans explained that it was a period that they called *shiva* (mourning).

"We have way too much food," Hans said to Adam and Evan. "Everybody who comes to the *shiva* will bring something to eat. It's a custom. This way the mourners don't have to concern themselves, and the house will have enough food for everyone. Please feel free to take some food home for your dinner. You'll be doing us a favor. I know a lot will be wasted, but this way, less food will go down the drain."

Barry added, "We'll be staying here for a few days. We don't want Ben to be alone so please come over often."

"Of course," Evan said, as he and Adam got up to leave. "We'll see you later. Maybe we'll have dinner here with you tonight."

"Great," Hans said and he kissed both Adam and Evan on the lips in front of all the company. As they left the Richter's, Billy Bingham ran after them.

"Hey fellas, hold up a sec, will you," he called after them. "Can I come in for a minute? I want to talk to you about a problem I'm having."

"Sure," Evan said. The three went into the house and Billy sat right down on the sofa. Adam sat next to him.

"Can I get you something?" Evan asked. Billy shook his head so Evan sat down on an easy chair facing the sofa." He and Adam looked at Billy. It was his ball game.

"I want to tell you something," Billy started.

"Wait," Evan said. "Is this something you should be telling your parents first?"

"Yes, but I can't," Billy almost screamed out. "After I tell you guys, please help me to tell them."

Adam's first thought was that Billy was going to come out to them. But that seemed absurd. He had known the young man since he was practically a toddler. Surely some of his gaydar would have warned him. No, he was going to tell them that he wanted to quit school. If that was it, he and Evan would do their best to talk him out of it.

"Talk fast before I burst," Adam demanded.

"I think I'm gay," Billy said and he dropped his head.

So Adam was right in what he thought this was about. Evan stood up from the easy chair and positioned himself in front of Billy. He asked, "What do you mean, you think? Don't you know?"

"Of course I know," Billy said emphatically. "I guess I was trying to leave a tightly sealed door a little bit ajar."

Finally Adam asked, "Aside from masturbation fantasies have you....?" He couldn't quite finish the sentence.

Billy nodded. "Many times," he said. "I have a boyfriend up at school. He wanted to come down here with me, but I told him it would be best if he wasn't around when I told my folks."

"Why are you afraid to tell them?" Evan asked. "They have always been very open minded about these things. Your father even went with us and Ben when we confronted those bozos who painted 'faggots' on our front door."

"I know. It's easy to be liberal when it doesn't concern you. Remember, I'm an only child and I'm sure they dream of spoiling grandchildren someday."

"The only thing I can advise is that you tell them as soon as possible," Evan said.

"I'm sure that's very wise," Adam said. "I was going to wait until after graduation when we moved away, but due to circumstances beyond our control, we came out just before graduation. I wanted to wait because I thought I'd be disowned. I was foolish and very wrong."

"That's funny," Billy said. "Fred and I will graduate in June. It's only two months away. We made the same decision as you did, Adam. We'll tell our folks after graduation and we are applying for work in New York, Los Angeles and San Francisco. We haven't heard anything yet, but we are confident."

"Tell them now!" Evan said sternly.

Adam was stirred from his memories when he heard a voice say, "Adam, I am so sorry." He looked up to see a handsome man in his early sixties holding out his hand and crying.

It took Adam a second to focus in on the man's face. It was someone he hadn't seen in many years, but had been in constant touch with.

"Billy! Billy," Adam said. "How wonderful it is to see you."

"You two can talk later," Jamie said. "They are calling us into the chapel."

Adam went through the service in a near fog. It was like his body was there but his mind was elsewhere. He caught glimmers of himself frolicking on the beach with Evan, holding his hand in a movie, making love in the shower, fighting about some idiotic minutia. Jamie sat on his right and Billy sat on his left. They stood him up at the proper time and took him to the limo. Billy told Jamie that he had taken a cab from the airport and had no transportation so he went with Adam and Jamie to the cemetery in the limo.

The service at graveside was short and sweet. When the casket was lowered, Adam maintained control, but when he tossed the first handful of dirt into the open cavern, he collapsed, and Billy and Jamie had to stand him up.

The only thing Adam could remember about the ride home was Jamie asking him if he was up to going to the dining room at Sunnydale." Yes," Adam answered. "I must. I'll be all right if you and Billy will stay beside me."

"Of course," they both answered together.

The miracle of the memorial luncheon was that Steve Baron actually came over to Adam to express his condolences. Steve was really expressing his relief that at last there would be no more queer hanky panky going on at his independent living facility. Upon reflection, he thought to himself that there were no other gays living there that he was aware of.

When the dining room staff started to clean up, Adam said that he would like to go to his apartment. "I don't want to slight you, Jamie," he said, "but it's been a lifetime since I have seen Billy. Would you mind if he came back with me?"

"Not at all," Jamie answered. "I want to get out of this monkey suit anyway."

Billy took Adam's arm. The two old friends smiled at each other and headed for Adam's place.

"How did you find out about Evan?" Adam asked Billy.

"Your friend Jamie called me. He said that he was calling everyone in your telephone directory, and that there weren't that many people to call."

"He's right," Adam lamented. "Most of my friends have passed away. It was so difficult to remove your mother's name when you wrote to tell me that she died last year. Pretty soon, there will be nobody left to remove and somebody will be removing me."

"Yes," Billy said. "It is sad. I can't tell you how many friends Fred and I lost to AIDS in the eighties. I thank God that we were a couple and monogamous."

"How is Fred?" Adam asked.

"He's great, but since he became a state senator we hardly see each other anymore. I fly up to Sacramento every other weekend. It's really hard."

They seated each other comfortably in the living room. Adam smiled broadly at Billy. "It is so wonderful to see you again after all these years," he said.

"Fred will be home for a couple of weeks in August," Billy informed Adam. "Why don't you fly out to LA and spend a couple of weeks with us. We would love to have you. And it's a lot cooler in LA in August than in Ft. Lauderdale, if I remember correctly."

"I believe you remember correctly. That sounds like a wonderful idea. I'll give it some serious thought. After your dad died, and your mother moved out there, Evan and I had every intention of paying you a visit, but something always came up to spoil our plans. That reminds me. Where are you staying?"

"I checked into a motel near the airport. I'm leaving tomorrow early in the morning, so it's good enough."

"Do you remember Sarah's funeral?" Adam asked. "You were so afraid to tell your folks that you were gay. It turned out just fine, didn't it? They were disappointed about the grandchildren thing, but they never stopped loving you or supporting you."

"They sure did. They made a big barbeque the first weekend after graduation so they could meet Fred. You were there, Ben Richter and Hans and Barry. I was the happiest guy in the world then. I had so many friends who had been disowned, but I was lucky. My parents still loved me. When Fred's folks said they wanted nothing to do with him, my folks made him their own."

"They were very special people," Adam commented. "But you moved away anyway."

"We didn't want to, but we both landed terrific jobs in LA and we had to do it."

"It was sad for all of us when you moved, but Evan and I had done the same thing so I had to be supportive too. Please stay and have dinner with me, just the two of us. I know a great restaurant nearby. We can walk over," Adam said.

"Of course. That would be wonderful, but I'll have to leave right after dinner."

CHAPTER FIVE

As he was finishing his shrimp cocktail appetizer, Billy asked. "Can you fill me in on a story I've heard lots about, but I never got any of the details?"

"What's that?" Adam asked.

"Well, how did Hans and Ben Richter identify the bigots who painted 'faggots' on your front door? Also I never heard what happened when you guys and my dad went over to confront them. I was too young to know about it then, and when my dad started to tell me the story years later, we somehow got interrupted by something and I never got the whole account."

Adam began, "Ben and Hans told me that when the Nazi guards came to round up the Jews and the homosexuals to take them to the 'showers' (which of course was a euphemism for 'gas chambers,') they always had sweet as apple pie smiles on their faces. They would grin and tell those poor souls to strip for the baths. They would then march them to the showers smiling and singing all the way. Well, you can bet those two guys knew a real smile from a phony one and that's how they were able to spot the Grangers right away.

"The Grangers lived at the end of the street. You won't remember them because they moved shortly after we confronted them. They were a father and a son. Rumor had it that their wife and mother had disappeared one night to avoid further physical abuse by her husband. It was just a rumor mind you. Nobody knew for sure.

"Several weeks after the incident, Hans came to me with a report from a detective agency he had hired to investigate them. It seems that Robert Granger, Sr. had been active in the German Bund prior to the war. He had been a well-known sympathizer to the Nazi cause. He and his wife never had children. He was always physically abusive to her, and finally she left him. Robert, Jr. was not a blood relative. The detective did not know how the two met, but one day Junior just moved in.

"The two of them had moved to our street just six months before Evan and I did. Why they never bothered the Richters, I'll never know. Maybe it was because they were living on our street first. Maybe it was because they and Hans could attest to the holocaust, which the Grangers were heard to say never happened. Whatever the reason, they chose to vent their hatred on us.

"So one Saturday morning, when we knew that both of them were home from work, Evan and I, your dad, Ben, Hans and Barry marched over and knocked on their door. They must have been scared shitless when they saw all us big guys standing there. Senior answered the door. He had a robe on and obviously nothing underneath. At first he registered shock. Then came the phony smile. We didn't wait for an invitation to enter. We just pushed past him. It never occurred to us that we were trespassing, and they could have had us all arrested.

"This was before videotapes were invented. We got a real shock when we rushed in to the house. There was a male porno film showing on a movie screen. Junior was lying on the couch naked sporting a rather impressive hard-on. It was obvious to all, that the phony father and son were homosexual lovers. Imagine the hypocrisy.

"Hans was our spokesman. He really reamed into them. Among a million other threats, he threatened to out them to the community and to their employers. We left that house laughing and in a complete state of disbelief. Within a week, they were gone and nobody knew where they went and nobody cared. The house remained empty and the lawn became an unsightly mess. The police feared that they might be dead inside so they got a warrant and broke in. The contents of the house were intact, but all their clothes were gone. The interesting thing is that the police found an equal amount of male pornography and Nazi propaganda. Eventually the house was repossessed by the bank. They cleaned it up and it was eventually sold to a lovely newlywed couple. Ironically, they were Jewish."

Adam started to laugh and Billy laughed too. "Yes, of course," he said. The Levy's lived there."

After dinner, Billy walked Adam back to his apartment. He called for a cab from there, and before he left, he begged Adam to come for that long awaited visit to Los Angeles. "If you think the trip is too much for you, maybe your friend Jamie would like to come too to help you out. I'd gladly pay for his expenses."

Before taking off, Billy knocked on Jamie's door to say goodbye and once again he offered Jamie an invitation to come with Adam for an all-expense paid vacation in LA.

"Wow, that's certainly an offer to consider," Jamie said. "I promise to give it serious thought and discuss it with Adam."

Before retiring, Jamie looked in on Adam. "How are you doing, fella?" he asked.

"Do you need anything?"

"It's been a long tough day, but I'm OK now. Billy's visit somehow revitalized me."

"I can see that," Jamie said, "and that's a good reason for us to consider that trip to LA come August. I'll talk to you about it tomorrow. You get to sleep now."

Adam brushed his teeth and then stripped. He climbed into bed and thought. *Well, the worst is over. The fear of seeing Evan put into the ground and covered up is over now. All that remains is for me to learn how to live without Evan at my side.* He wondered if he could. He didn't think it would be possible.

As Adam began to doze off, he began to feel uneasy. Suddenly he was racked with guilt. He remembered back to a time when he had cheated on Evan. Afterwards, he had agonized whether he should confess to Evan or let it drop. In the end he did not tell Evan. The years passed and he forgot all about it, but the thought of it would recur at odd moments.

He, Evan and Eve were chatting and drinking at a table in The Male Room. They were waiting for Eve's partner to arrive. Suddenly Adam felt Eve's hand on his thigh. He thought Eve might be groping him, but he realized that all she was trying to do was put something into his pocket. He moved slightly to accommodate her. When the task was done, Eve brought her hand back on top of the table.

Tom Peterson finally arrived, and Adam and Evan were surprised. Tom was at least thirty years older than Eve, well into his sixties. Yet he was lean and virile looking and very, very handsome. After the introductions were made, Eve looked at Adam and said, "You'll love this Adam. Tom picked me up on the subway a couple of years ago and I went home with him. The rest is for the history books." Tom looked inquisitive so Eve filled him in on how he had picked Adam up on a subway and taken his virginity. Adam blushed a deep crimson.

They all had a couple of drinks together and then went their separate ways. As soon as they got to their apartment, Adam rushed to the bathroom. He removed a card from his pocket. It was Eve's. It read "Evan Fury" and contained his phone number. Eve had written on the card: *Please call. Let's have some fun.* Adam placed the card in his wallet.

Evan had a final exam early the next morning. As soon as he was gone, Adam called Eve. They began a conspiracy.

Adam said he would tell Evan that he had to go to New Brunswick on Sunday. He would tell him that he wouldn't be long, and he should remain in their apartment and study for the remaining final exam. Eve told him that he would reserve a room at a hotel near the campus and they could spend the day together. All this happened at the wrong time. Adam could hardly concentrate on his exams. All he could think about was being with Eve. He wasn't even feeling guilty.

He thought Sunday would never come. Evan kissed him goodbye as he left and reminded him to be back early to study for their last final exam the next day. Adam assured him that he would.

He reached the hotel and looked around before going in. He asked the clerk for Evan Fury's room number and ran up the stairs rather than use the elevator. He rapped loudly on the door. The door opened and strong arms dragged him inside. Eve was naked and he quickly closed and bolted the door. He was all over Adam and stripped him rapidly. All the while he was removing Adam's clothes, he was kissing him passionately.

When Adam was naked, Eve took a good look at him. My God you have filled out and matured," Eve said. "You are gorgeous." He pulled Adam down on the bed and went down on him. Adam had dreamed of this moment for six years, and for the past week the thought of this moment had obsessed him. He came quickly, and Eve swallowed his spunk hungrily.

When he calmed down, he rolled Eve over and proceeded to suck his cock. Eve took a little longer to gush down Adam's throat, but not by much. Afterward the two lay side by side, catching their breaths.

"That was fantastic," Eve said. Adam wanted to agree but he couldn't. He realized that what had just happened was pure lust. There wasn't an iota of love in it.

I've been a fucking idiot, Adam thought. *I love you so much, Evan. Why did I ever do this? I must be out of my mind.*

"Do you think we can get in one fuck apiece before you leave?" Eve asked.

"Gee, I'm really sorry, but I have a final exam in the morning and I told Evan I'd get home early so we could study together." Adam jumped up and got dressed rapidly.

"It's been great," he said. He gave Eve a quick kiss and ran out of the room and back to Evan. He never saw Eve again, nor did he want to. Unfortunately, the remembrance of the incident would come to him at odd times, and he would be racked with guilt. He prayed often that Evan would never find out. As far as he knew Evan never did. He felt sure that Evan would have forgiven him anyway, if he had ever found out.

———————

Surprisingly, Adam slept well all night. When the sunlight poured into his room and awakened him, he felt truly rested. He was also surprised that he felt surprisingly at peace. The funeral had provided some closure for him. Evan was gone and he had to come to grips with it. He dialed Jamie's number and told him that he would meet him in the dining room for breakfast. Then he hopped out of bed and started his morning routine.

For the first time in more than sixty years, Adam was a single man, and he swore to adjust to it for whatever time he had left. He was healthy, and although Jamie drove him around, he was perfectly capable of getting around on his own. He was also aware that there were many senior groups that met on a regular basis at the GLCC. He vowed to check some of them out. He and Evan had attended a gay church intermittently, and he decided to go more often and meet new people.

At breakfast he told Jamie about his not so New Year resolutions and Jamie was pleased as punch.

"Good for you," he said. "I was truly worried about you, but I feel better now. Any chance some of those groups you are talking about would let in a token straight guy? They sound like fun. I wouldn't mind going to church with you. I haven't gone in years."

"I'm sure it can happen," Adam said. "They wouldn't dare allow themselves to be accused of discrimination, now would they?"

"Speaking of gay men, that Billy Bingham friend of yours sure is a handsome dude. Tell me about him."

"There's not much to tell. He grew up next door to us. Evan and I adored him. He was the son we would never have. I guess Billy felt the same way. He was always coming over to hang out with us. When he was a young boy, it was fine, but when he continued to hang out with us when he was in high school, we should have suspected something. Neither Evan nor I ever had the least suspicion that Billy was gay. He certainly never confided in us until he had been in a relationship for over three years. When he did come out to us we were as shocked as everyone. I think he looked to us to be there for him in case his folks didn't support him. He didn't have to worry. His parents loved him too much. His partner Fred's folks disowned him, and the Binghams treated Fred like their own son.

"When the boys moved to LA, we were devastated. We saw each other off and on in the early years, but after some time, they just stopped visiting their folks in Florida. Instead, the parents began to take an annual vacation in California. We often talked about the four of us going together, but it somehow never happened. It's something I'll always regret."

"Then I think we should plan to go this coming August," Jamie said.

"Yes, and I intend to call Billy at least once a week from now on. Aside from you, he's the only family I have left."

Jamie was very moved that Adam considered him to be family. After breakfast they parted. Adam put on a swimsuit and went down to the pool. He wanted to soak up some warm sun. He found a lounge chair and sat down facing the sun. He put a towel across his legs and closed his eyes.

_____

"We should plan a trip to LA to visit Billy and Fred," Adam said.

"Sure, no problem, if you can figure out when," Evan replied. "Since I became volunteer coordinator at the GLCC, I can't put two weeks together without some activity requiring my attention."

"They got along without you in the past, and they'll get along without you for two weeks in the present," Adam replied, very peeved. "Never mind going to Los Angeles, we haven't had any vacation time since you volunteered your services over there."

"I know, I know. But I can't get anyone to assist me and take over for a few days."

Adam shook his head sadly. "These young guys are only interested in the bars, booze, drugs and sex. Service is a word that just isn't in their vocabularies."

"You're right, but think of it this way. They'll get older someday too, and then maybe they'll think about service to their communities."

"If they survive their hedonism," Adam commented sarcastically.

So the years flew by and they still didn't ever visit Los Angeles. Now Billy's parents and Evan were all gone. *No more procrastinating*, Adam resolved. This afternoon, during lunch, he and Jamie would sit down and plan when they could go out west. Then he would call Billy and Fred and make sure the dates were good with them.

At lunch he discussed his resolve with Jamie who couldn't be more supportive and enthusiastic.

"I was stationed in San Diego for a while when I was in the navy, and I haven't gone back out west since then," Jamie informed Adam. "I'll bet it's changed a ton."

After lunch, they took out their calendars. "Billy said that we should come in August when Fred would be home for two weeks, but I never asked him when in August," Adam lamented.

"I'll bet it's the last two weeks, and he'll be home until after the Labor Day holiday," Jamie suggested. "Anyway, it doesn't matter. I have no pressing engagements during August or the Labor Day Weekend."

"I think I can clear my calendar also, if I have to," Adam said, and he started to laugh. Jamie was so pleased. It was the first time

Adam had laughed since Evan died. That evening Adam called Billy and arranged for a visit the last week of August through Labor Day. Billy was delighted, but he was sorry that the visit was more than three months away, and for such a short time.

Over the next two weeks, Jamie and Adam busied themselves making travel arrangements, and checking the average temperatures in LA at that time of year, so they could decide what clothing to pack.

Finally Jamie said, "This is crazy. We aren't going to Siberia. If we have to buy some clothing there in order to be appropriate, so be it." Adam agreed.

Adam and Evan were homebodies. Neither of them cared much for travel. That might explain why they had really never gotten up the energy to visit Billy and Fred all these years. About the only trip they had ever made was on a gay cruise out of Port Everglades. They were in their seventies then, and as much as they enjoyed the eye candy, they really didn't participate much in the on board activities. They enjoyed the company of the much younger people at their dining table, but not enough to see them again. They, Hans and Barry had talked about doing a trip like this for years, but somehow they never did. Hans and Barry were gone by the time Adam and Evan finally decided to take the cruise.

Thinking back on it, Adam concluded that he and Evan had been too much in love, and had not needed other people in their lives. Consequently they had not made any really close buddies except Hans and Barry. *Well, it's too late to change now*, Adam thought, *and thank God for Jamie.* For the first time he wished that Jamie was gay so that he could attend some gay events with him. But hadn't Jamie asked to join him anyhow? One of the gay senior groups was having a Memorial Day picnic and Adam decided to ask Jamie if he would like to go.

"You don't think I'd let you go alone," Jamie joked. "Why those horny vultures would be all over you. So I have to be there to protect you."

"Very funny," Adam quipped back. "What if I want them all over me?" They both laughed heartily.

In the end Jamie went to two gay picnics with Adam, and he had a good time. The first was the Memorial Day Picnic and the second was the July 4th picnic. Jamie met someone at the Memorial Day picnic who looked familiar to him. He thought it might be an old high school acquaintance named Tim Dougherty. He encountered him and it was indeed Tim from high school.

"Christ," Tim said, "I wish I knew you were gay back then. I would have been more interested in you."

"Cool down," Jamie said. "I'm not gay. I'm just kind of enjoying taking care of Adam." Jamie and Tim spent a lot of time revisiting their high school days, and Tim came to visit him and Adam at The Sunnydale House a couple of times before July 4th.

They all met up again at the July 4th picnic. Again Tim and Jamie were lost in conversation. At one point, Adam asked Jamie jokingly if he was thinking of switching teams. "The sex is really good," Adam advised Jamie.

To which Jamie answered rather cryptically. "At my age it might be a good thing to try everything at least once before it's too late." Then he went right back to Tim leaving Adam talking to other friends. Since Evan's death, Adam had joined a couple of senior groups and was making more gay friends than he had ever had before, and so was Jamie who accompanied him everywhere.

Adam was even more curious when Jamie told him that Tim was coming to The Sunnydale House to have dinner with them Saturday evening. After dinner there was a free movie at the facility which they could all enjoy.

Adam might have been old, but there was nothing wrong with his night vision. In the darkened theater, he glanced over to Jamie who was sitting on his right. Tim was sitting to the right of Jamie. Tim's hand was on Jamie's crotch and he was clearly massaging it. Jamie's hand was reaching over to Tim, but Adam could not see where it landed.

Smiling to himself, he leaned over to Jamie and whispered, "I'm not enjoying this movie and I'm rather tired. Excuse me now. I'm going to my apartment. Please say goodnight to Tim for me."

Once back in his apartment, he listened intently to any sounds he might hear from next door. Less than five minutes later, he distinctly heard Jamie's door open and then close. Very shocked, but extremely happy at what might be going on, Adam retired for the night. Try as hard as he could, Adam could not hear anything coming from next door.

As soon as Jamie locked the door behind them, Tim asked, "Are you sure you want to do this?"

"Yes, I'm sure," Jamie answered. "Aren't you?"

Tim smiled. "Damn sure," he said.

"How do we go about it?" Jamie asked, a wee bit bewildered.

Tim laughed. "Let's just sit down on the sofa, hold hands and talk." He led Jamie to the sofa and they sat side by side. Their bodies were touching.

"I hope this won't gross you out, but just like with heterosexuals, we usually start by kissing and petting. The kissing may gross you out this first time, but once you get into it and start tonguing your partner, the rest comes easier."

"Shouldn't we get undressed?" Jamie asked in all innocence.

"We will, in time. Don't rush it. I'm not going anywhere. We have all night." That having been said, Tim leaned into Jamie and planted a chaste kiss on his lips. At the same time, he placed a hand on Jamie's knee. After the kiss he pulled away and smiled at Jamie who looked scared shitless.

"Relax," Tim said and he leaned into Jamie again. This time he kissed him with his lips parted. Jamie was astounded how nice the kiss felt. It was just like any kiss he had ever shared with a woman. He kissed back, parting his lips. Involuntarily he placed a hand on Tim's thigh.

"That's it," Tim said. "Relax and enjoy." With that, he forced his tongue into Jamie's mouth, which turned out to be a ready receptacle. As their kissing became more passionate, Tim's hand went further up Jamie's knee until he found the crotch which Jamie had willingly given him in the darkened movie theater.

Jamie made a little moaning sound, encouraging Tim to proceed. He undid Jamie's belt and pulled down the zipper. He slipped his hand under Jamie's shorts and grasped his growing cock. Until then no man had ever touched Jamie there. It was the sole property of his wife and the few women he had fucked along the way. Tim gently stroked Jamie's cock with a feathery touch. Jamie was glad to note that it was as good as any woman's touch.

"Aaah," Jamie let out an involuntary sigh. "That feels so nice."

"Wouldn't you like to do that to me?" Tim asked. He let loose of Jamie and pulled down his own pants and boxer shorts, allowing Jamie full access. Jamie stared at Tim's erect missile. It was neither too large nor too small, and Jamie stared at it much too long before finally getting up the courage to take it in his hand, It felt so soft on the outside and so hard beneath the skin. Jamie was pleased that it was such a nice feeling.

"Now that we are both hard," Tim said, "let's get undressed and give your bed a work out." He pulled up his pants so as not to trip. They both scurried into the bedroom and undressed rapidly. When they were naked, Tim grabbed hold of Jamie. He rubbed their bodies together, and resumed kissing Jamie with his mouth open and his tongue hungry to find Jamie's.

"Lie on your back," Tim said gently to Jamie. Jamie did just that, but instinctively he set his feet wide apart. Tim lay down on top of him and resumed the kissing. He reached underneath them and began to stroke Jamie's cock.

"God," Jamie muttered. "It's been forever since anyone touched me there." He reached underneath and found Tim's cock which he enveloped in his fist. Tim was happy but shocked. He expected Jamie to be more reticent. This was a turning point in the love making and in Jamie's life. At this moment, Jamie became a full participant. He was no longer passive.

Tim could sense Jamie's hunger and he scooted down until he was breathing on Jamie's pulsating cock. He held Jamie's testicles in one hand and grasped his cock with the other. He pulled down the foreskin and began to lick Jamie's purple head. He felt Jamie recoil, but he knew that it wasn't from the blow job, but from a too sensitive head. Tim had been with many men who could not bear to have the head stimulated. He took Jamie's cock fully into his mouth and Jamie totally relaxed. Tim's tongue began to lick up and down Jamie's shaft. Every so often, he released it and he licked Jamie's balls. At those times, Jamie lifted his buttocks trying to force more of his balls into Tim's mouth.

Jamie was thinking that Adam was right. The sex was fantastic, but at his age it was taking him a long time to cum. He couldn't help thinking that in his youth he would have cum twice already. He wondered if Tim would have the stamina to bring him to climax. He didn't have to wonder long. Suddenly the feeling he was feeling refreshed his memory. He was beginning to feel that undeniable pleasure. "Please don't stop," he stuttered to Tim. Tim had no intention of stopping. He felt Jamie's balls shriveling, and knew that he was close.

Jamie gushed into Tim's mouth. He hadn't had an orgasm in a very long time, but even so, he did not produce much sperm. Tim kept right on sucking and Jamie had to beg him to stop. "My head is too sensitive," he informed Tim while he was gasping for air.

Tim scooted up the bed and lay side by side with Jamie. He put his hand gently on Jamie's diminished cock. Tim had devoured every drop of Jamie's juices and Jamie was perfectly clean.

"Do you think that you could do that to me?" Tim asked. Before Jamie could answer, Tim said. "If it would gross you out, do you think you could at least whack me off?" Jamie turned to Tim and put his finger on Tim's mouth to silence him.

"I've gone this far," he said. "Do you think I'm going to chicken out now?" He leaned over and took Tim's very hard cock into his mouth.

The next morning Adam pondered whether or not he should call Jamie about breakfast. In the end, he decided to call him. If he didn't call, he reasoned, Jamie would know that Adam knew that Tim had gone to his apartment the night before. As he reached for the phone, it rang. It was Jamie who told him that he would be over in five minutes. He also told Adam that he wanted to talk to him for a few minutes before they went to breakfast. Adam could well imagine what he wanted to talk about and practiced being surprised or shocked or whatever.

There was a knock on the door, and Adam let Jamie in. Jamie sat right down on a chair in the living room. "I had sex with Tim last night," he blurted out. "Male sex!"

"And??"

"It was wonderful. All of it, and I don't feel guilty or dirty or anything. I feel good."

"How about Tim?" Adam asked.

"He just left a few minutes ago. He said I was great and he wants us to see more of each other. Do you mind?"

Adam began to laugh. "Of course not. Now we can all go to gay events together, and you don't have to feel like an outsider."

"I've got news for you," Jamie said. "I never did feel like an outsider."

CHAPTER SIX

With two weeks left before their trip to California, Adam told himself to stop procrastinating and get himself ready. Billy said that he and Fred had one guest room, which Adam could use, and that their third bedroom was furnished as an office, but it had a sleep sofa in it for Jamie.

Tim was regretful that he wasn't going along. He and Jamie were becoming inseparable, and Jamie was considering moving out of The Sunnydale House and moving in with Tim. This made Adam sad, but at the same time Jamie's happiness was important to him and in the end he gave Jamie his blessing.

"Don't worry," they assured Adam. "We'll pick you up for every event, and you can stay in our guest room any time you want to stay over." Very gingerly, Tim asked Adam to ask Billy if he would mind if Jamie's boyfriend could come along and share the sleep sofa.

Reluctantly Adam made the call. He was afraid Billy wouldn't want the extra company.

"I thought Jamie was straight," Billy said.

"I guess he fooled us all," Adam replied.

"Of course, he can come. We'll have a blast."

Tim could not get on their outgoing flight, but he was able to book a ticket on another airline, and would arrive within an hour of Jamie and Adam. They would wait for him at the airport in LA. He was able to obtain a seat on their return flight.

About a week before their departure. Adam got up on a chair so that he could reach way back on the shelf of his walk in bedroom closet. There were two rarely used suitcases stored there. Neither was tremendously large, and he was determined to fit everything in one suitcase so that he wouldn't be burdened carrying two.

One suitcase had his name tag on it, and the other had Evan's. He wasn't certain why, but he decided to take Evan's suitcase. He had to change the address on the name tag anyway, and besides that, it was lying on top of his. He laid the case in the corner of his bedroom and two more days passed before he opened it. When he did, he got quite a surprise. There was a diary lying in the suitcase. It had an old fashioned clasp, but it wasn't locked. It had to be Evan's.

Adam removed the journal, but hesitated to open it. He felt that it might be a violation of Evan's privacy, but he and Evan had never had any secrets from each other, so he decided to open the book.

Again he hesitated. He had kept his rendez-vous with Eve a secret, hadn't he? What if Adam had some secrets he shouldn't know about? Is it proper for him to find out now that Evan was dead?

He pondered the imponderable and finally opened the book. There were very few entries for a journal spanning four years. The flyleaf read:

My College Years
Evan Morrissey
1946-1950

It took Adam more mental agonizing to turn to the first entry:

May 23, 1946: *It came in the mail today! Oh joy! I have been accepted to NYU. I hope I get a hot roommate and he's a homo. Why waste a good thing?*

Adam laughed to himself.

Sept. 5, 1946: *What a day! My dad had to double park on a busy street for us to unload my junk. Maybe I should have gone to a country school. We got my stuff into my room and Dad took off quickly before he got a ticket. I wonder when I'll get to Long Island again.*

My roommate was almost unpacked when we arrived. We introduced ourselves, and he helped me settle in. His name is Mark Clare. He's a couple of years older than I, and he just got out of the navy. Unless my gaydar is totally defective, I'm sure he's hetero, very hetero. Bummer!

Sept. 6, 1946: *We had to sit through a boring
orientation today. Who cares? NYU advertises
that all of New York City is its campus. That
should be good enough, especially with Greenwich
Village right next door.*

*Some cute blond kid sat down right in front of me.
When I saw him, I could feel my cock stirring. I've
got to meet him and I hope he's gay or at least
gay friendly, horny and easily persuaded to switch
teams.*

After reading that, Adam was shocked. When he met Evan at
The Male Room, Evan pretended to think hard where they knew each
other from. He was putting on an act. God love him. Adam began
to cry.

His phone rang shrilly. It was Jamie. "Tim's here," he said.
"We're going out to dinner. Want to join us?"

"Not tonight," Adam answered. I'm all wrapped up in things.
You two have a good time. I love you both."

"We love you too. I'll see you tomorrow morning, if I make
it to breakfast." Jamie was moving out the day before the trip, and
Adam was sad to think about it. He went back to the journal.

Sept. 9, 1946: *Classes started today. There are
some cute guys in some of my classes, but my
gaydar says straight, straight, straight. My last
class of the day is English Lit. The cute blond boy
is in it. We both sit in the third row at opposite
ends. I found out that his name is Adam Langston,
but I'm still not sure which way he swings. I'll
have to be very observant. Should I approach him*

or try to learn more about him? I think I should wait. He's one of the few non veterans on campus and he seems out of place and uncomfortable. I don't want to scare him away so I'll bide my time.

After I wrote the above, I went to shower. Adam was there. I don't think he saw me, but I took a good look at him. He has the most beautiful ram rod I've ever seen. I've got to get that thing in my mouth and up my ass. It's so delicious looking.

Adam could not believe what he was reading, reading with pleasure. He had no idea that Evan felt this way about him before they had met officially.

Sept. 30, 1946: *The Semester is almost a month old and I still can't figure Adam out. I have been watching him. He hasn't hit on any girls or any boys either. Because he is so insecure, he's holding back. I wish he'd make a move so I could get a clue. I don't want to do anything to scare him away, but I want to make love to him desperately.*

Oct. 1, 1946. 3 AM: *So here's what happened after I wrote the above words. I happened to go to the bathroom. On my way back, I saw Adam. He was wearing a cardigan sweater and he was going out. I grabbed a sweater also and followed him. He was headed toward The Village. When he got there he wandered aimlessly. Finally when he passed The Male Room, he looked in and I got my hopes up, but he walked on by. I continued to follow him. My underwear was full of precum just looking at him*

Then a miracle happened. He turned around and went into the bar. I wanted to cry with joy. He is a homo. I followed discreetly and saw him take a seat at the far end of the bar. I waited until his back was turned away from the entrance and I went in. I bought a drink and then I approached him casually. I pretended that I couldn't think where I knew him from, but he looked familiar. He said the same thing. Finally I identified myself as a fellow English Lit student. We found a seat. I bought him a drink. We danced. When I could stand it no longer, I invited him back to my room.

He was practically a virgin, but we made passionate love. His cock is the tastiest I have ever had in my mouth, and when it was up my ass it was a perfect fit. We are made for each other, and I told him how much I love him. He told me he loves me too. I can't believe it. I have never felt such joy in my life.

He is sleeping in my bed as I write these words. I swear. I'll never let him sleep in anyone else's bed as long as I live.

Adam groaned as he remembered his indiscretion with Eve. He wished with all his heart that he could erase it.

The next entry was sometime later:

Dec.15, 1946: *Mark told me that he's leaving after the semester. He's moving to California where he has wanted to live since he was stationed there in the Navy. I rushed down to the housing office and arranged for Adam to move in with me. I can't wait to see the look on his face when I tell him. It's been tough finding places to make love. Our problem is solved. Hallelujah!*

Aug. 15, 1947: *I am so happy. Adam and I just signed a lease on a studio apartment in Greenwich Village. It's a stone's throw away from The Male Room, and a short walk to school. Outside of a cold dorm room, it's our first home together, our own little love nest. We take possession on Sept.1. I can't wait.*

Nov. 20, 1949: *Adam and I have agreed to spend holidays at our parents. They are aware that we are roommates and best friends. We are going to New Brunswick for Thanksgiving and to Oceanside for Christmas. Neither of the folks seemed to mind it at all. I wonder if they suspect something. Sometimes I wish they would find out so we can get the big reveal over with. I wasn't as afraid of facing the Nazis as I am of facing my folks with the news that I am queer.*

Nov. 26, 1949: *We had Thanksgiving dinner at The Langston's this afternoon. They couldn't have been nicer to me if I was their own son. I wonder if they suspect the truth about Adam and me. If they do they sure didn't give any indication.*

Adam shuddered when he thought back to that Christmas.

Dec. 26, 1949: Adam and I arrived early on Christmas morning and attended church with my parents and my kid brother. When we got home everyone pitched in getting dinner ready. Finally my mother kicked us guys out of the kitchen. We sat down in the living room with my dad and were just shooting the breeze when I asked Adam to please pass me the fruit bowl or just hand me an apple. Without thinking, I called him "honey."

My dad sat bolt upright in his chair. He searched both our faces as we tried to ignore the whole thing. He demanded to know if there was anything sexual going on between us, and throwing caution to the winds, I threw my arms around Adam's shoulders and told my dad that we were soul mates and lovers. I could write a volume about what happened next, but long story short, we were kicked out of the house. My brother tried to intervene, but my dad threatened to kick him out too.

Adam tried to console me on the LIRR train back to the city, but I was inconsolable. When we reached Penn Station, we transferred to the Pennsylvania RR and took a train to New Brunswick. Adam insisted that now he had to tell his parents. We waited almost three hours for the train because they were on a holiday schedule.

When we got to Adam's parents they were just ending their holiday meal and they were very surprised to see us. Mr. Langston said that he thought we were supposed to go to my parents. He looked perturbed at his mistake, but we assured him that he was correct.

I was shaking like a leaf and he asked me what was wrong, so as quick as a rabbit, for fear of losing his nerve, Adam came out with it.

Adam's parents looked at each other and Mrs. Langston said, "Adam darling, we've known for years that you are homosexual. We were just waiting for you to say so, and if you didn't want to tell us, we would have respected your decision." Then she turned to me. "Evan, I can't believe your parents threw you out. It's unfair, unkind and on Christmas Day, it's totally unchristian. You will always have a place in our home."

Adam's kid brothers, who are twins, Mike and Bob, embraced both of us. Mike even said that he always liked me and he was glad I was going to be his brother.

Now I am sorry that I have taken the job offer in Miami, but it is too good to turn down.

June 3, 1950: We have been studying nonstop so last night I talked Adam into taking a break and we went to The Male Room. The entertainer there turned out to be Eve, the guy who took Adam's virginity when he was sweet sixteen. He joined us after the show and I could see the longing in Adam's eye when they met. I also saw Eve slip him something under the table.

I know Adam wants to have sex with him. Your first experience always leaves lasting memories that you would like to relive. If I try to stop it, Adam might resent me. If I pretend not to notice, he'll get it out of his system. I know how much he loves me and I am secure in that knowledge. He'll always come home to me. I had plenty of guys before I met Adam. I can be big about it and let him have one more go at it.

June 7, 1950: Adam came home today much earlier than I expected. I guess his rendezvous with Eve didn't turn out as great as he had fantasized. We studied for our last final exam, but I could see how distracted he was. I made us take a break and we made love. I could tell from the love making that I had Adam back. He will always be mine. Eve is finally out of his system.

Adam was now sniveling. Evan knew about Eve all the time and never let on. No wonder he had loved him so much. *Evan, I miss you so much.*

Adam now turned to the last entry in the book.

June 15, 1950: *Well, Adam and I have our degrees. Adam's parents and brothers and my brother, Eddie, attended graduation ceremonies. Mr. Langston (he wants me to call him Dad) took us all out to dinner. Our bags are packed and stowed in the trunk of the old car I bought. We leave for Florida in the morning. Adam's parents were very weepy, but our brothers were excited. To them it's a major adventure and they can't wait to visit us someday.*

That was the end of the very short journal. Adam was amused at the old fashioned, politically incorrect references to gays. If Evan had ever started a new journal to record his post college days, Adam was unaware of it and wouldn't know where to look for it. The discovery of this diary was a miracle in itself. It was obvious that Evan was not into journalizing, but what he did record elated Adam's spirits. Now he knew for sure that Evan had fallen in love with him before they ever met. Now that he knew that Evan knew about Eve, he could give up feeling guilty about his indiscretion once and for all. He was actually happy.

Adam decided not to sit alone in his apartment, and went down to the dining room for dinner. He had been eating all his meals with Jamie for so long that he was at a loss where to sit. He looked around the room and spotted someone waving at him. It was Bernie Lang. Bernie was a widower and he and Jamie had often rounded out a bridge foursome with Evan and himself. He walked over to Bernie, who was eating alone.

"You're alone tonight for a change. Come, sit with me," Bernie invited Adam. "So where is Jamie?"

"He's having dinner out tonight with a friend," was all Adam would offer.

"I hear he's moving out at the end of the month. Too bad, I'll miss him. Maybe you and I can find a new bridge game," Bernie said.

"That will be wonderful," Adam lied, as the waitress came to take his order.

They were silent for a while. Then Bernie said, "Evan's funeral was beautiful. I'm sorry for your loss." Having said that, he looked down at his plate.

"Thanks," Adam mumbled.

"On a happier note," Bernie smiled, "today I went to the *bris* of my first great grandson. That's a ritual circumcision, you know."

"I know," Adam said. "Congratulations."

"Thank you," he answered. "Frankly I can't see how I can be eating anything tonight. My son and my grandson put out quite a spread, and naturally I gorged myself. In my old age I've lost all my will power."

"Don't sweat it," Adam said. "At our age all we have left is food, bathroom activities and sleep, if we are lucky."

"How right you are," Bernie agreed. After dinner Bernie talked Adam into going to the card room, where they actually got into a bridge game. Their opponents were way too good for them, and whipped them badly. They all agreed to end the game early.

Back in his apartment Adam thought back to another *bris,* a very long time ago.

One Sunday evening, shortly after the Granger incident, their phone rang and Evan answered it.

"It's Hans," Evan told Adam.

Usually a conversation with Hans consisted of a lot of back and forth banter, and lots of laughter, but Evan remained silent. He was listening intently to whatever Hans was telling him. Finally, he said, "You gotta be kidding. No shit! You bet. I'll see you at 6:30 in the morning."

"What?" Adam asked impatiently.

"Hans just got back from the airport. Barry is off to Chicago for a week on business. Hans wants to surprise him when he gets back, and he's getting circumcised tomorrow morning. We have to deliver him to the outpatient clinic at 7:30 AM. His rabbi will be there to recite the prayers to make it a ritual circumcision. He didn't ask Ben to drive him because he doesn't want Ben and Sarah to know until it's over and he's healed. One of us will pick him up at the end of the day and we are going to stay with him for a couple of days. I'll call my boss and tell him I need to take tomorrow off to tend a sick friend. Do you think you can take Tuesday off?"

"What if Barry wants to have an uncut cock to make love to. This is just plain crazy," Adam moaned.

"I know, but it's Hans's wish to be really and totally Jewish. Barry will have to respect his wishes. Start packing a bag for us for the couple of days. I need to make two calls."

Evan called Ben and told him that he and Adam were going to dog sit at a friend's house for two or three days and not to worry when they don't come home tomorrow. Then he called the Binghams and told them the truth of what was going on. Jack responded by groaning, and promising not to tell the Richters.

As it turned out, Evan and Adam were both able to pick Hans up because he was not released until 8 PM. He was taken to the car in a wheel chair and when they arrived at his house, he got out of the car and Adam burst out laughing. Hans was walking like a bow legged cowboy with a broom stick up his ass.

Hans gave him a dirty look. "Sorry!" Adam said, stifling further laughter.

Hans had on a bath robe with nothing underneath. Evan sat him on a recliner chair in the living room. His robe fell open and Evan could see Hans's cock covered with a gauze containing a couple of blood spots.

"How do you feel?" Evan asked.

"Not bad. It burns a little, but there's no real pain. I need to change the dressing in an hour or so. I'm a little scared."

"I'll help you," Adam volunteered. "I have never held a cut cock in my hands in my life."

"You have a gutter mind," Hans said. "The last thing on my mind right now is sex."

"Sorry," Adam said again. He tried to sober down, but for some reason the whole situation was amusing him.

Adam made them all coffee and found some chocolate chip cookies in the cupboard. "They're Ellie's," Hans said.

"No shit! I'd know them anywhere," Adam said.

After Evan cleaned up, Hans pointed to a paper bag he had been given at the clinic. "There's fresh gauze and a lubricant of some kind in the bag. For some reason I'm scared that the old gauze is sticking to the wound and I'm afraid to remove it. Adam, I'll take you up on your offer to change the bandage for me. Adam didn't really want to do it, but he had promised."

He gingerly lifted Hans' cock and cradled it in his palm. Carefully he began to remove the gauze which fortunately did not stick.

"So how does it feel to hold a cut cock in your hand?" Hans asked.

"Who knew? I don't feel any difference."

Adam took some lubricant and began to coat Hans's cock around the surgical wound. There were several small stitches, and Adam was afraid to touch them.

"The doctor says that they'll dissolve in a few days," Hans told him.

Suddenly Hans screamed. "Stop, stop Adam," he yelled. "I'll have to do it myself."

"Did I hurt you?" Adam asked in alarm.

"Hell no. I started to get hard, and it hurt like the blazes. You should have told me that Adam had a velvet touch, Evan." Hans was back to his jokes and banter.

Hans was never shy about anything. A few weeks later, in the middle of dinner at Hans and Barry's house, he suddenly jumped up, dropped his pants, and proudly displayed his fully healed, circumcised cock.

"And it still works fine," Barry attested. "I must admit, however, I kind of miss nibbling on his foreskin."

CHAPTER SEVEN

The big jet plane landed at LAX and roared to a stop. Adam and Jamie were seated almost in the rear, and it took them forever to deplane. In fact, by the time they got to the carousel, the luggage from their flight was already coming down the chute. They each had been able to get everything into one suitcase, so all either had with him was a carry on and a suitcase.

They had no problem wheeling their light load to another airline's carousel where they waited for Tim's plane to arrive. When the three of them were together, they took a shuttle bus to the car rental and rented a mid-size car. With the aid of directions supplied by Billy, and a navigation system, they started out to Billy's house.

Billy instructed them to get on one of LA's freeways. Before they were all the way up the entrance ramp, they were stalled in heavy traffic. Billy's instructions, supplied by Mapquest, said that the trip would take twenty-five minutes. After twenty-five minutes they still had not merged onto the freeway. They were not liking LA very much. In all, it took them one hour and fifty minutes to reach Billy's driveway.

Billy was at work, but he had told them where to find a key. He also told them to unpack and freshen up and he would be home at about 5:30. It was now 4:45. They each showered and changed and were all freshened when Billy did come home. He embraced Adam and Jamie and shook Tim's hand heartily.

"Fred should be home soon," he said. "He's at his local office. This is supposed to be his vacation, but he's working. As soon as he gets home, we'll go out to dinner."

Jamie and Tim were only four or five years older than Billy and Fred. Notwithstanding that they were contemporaries, they and Adam were accustomed to eating dinner no later than 6 PM. Fred did not get home until 8:40 PM. Back east in Florida it was 11:40 PM. The men were starving.

After greetings were over, Fred excused himself. He said that he needed to shower and change before dinner. At 9:40 PM they finally set out for dinner. They drove for about a half hour more before reaching their destination. The Floridians were amazed to find the restaurant overflowing, and the bar was three deep at this late hour. The wait would be at least three quarters of an hour.

"Maybe we should go elsewhere," Tim suggested.

"You'll find the same crowds at any decent restaurant," Fred said. "We might as well tough it out here." By this time the easterners were groggy with sleep and rapidly losing their appetites. Their appetites were refreshed when they finally got seated and saw the menu, which was mainly Caribbean. Everything was delicious and very expensive. Fred picked up the check and the visitors objected strongly.

"First night out is our treat," Billy said. "We can go Dutch after this. By the way, tomorrow we are planning on going to a gay bar and restaurant for dinner. The bar will be busier than the restaurant so we won't have as long a wait for dinner. Also we are both officially starting our vacations tomorrow until Labor Day. It will be tough to keep Fred away from his office. You guys will have to help me."

That night Adam slept like a log, but he awakened at 4:30 in the morning. His body clock was still on Eastern Time, where it was 7:30 AM. If he was home he would be going down to breakfast about now. He certainly wasn't hungry, but he needed to pee badly. Remembering that he was naked, he grabbed a robe and stepped out into the hall. Fred and Billy were to his right and Tim and Jamie were to his left. The bathroom was directly across the hall.

The hall was dark and quiet. He thought he heard sounds coming from Tim and Jamie's room. Yup! The two of them were going at it and they were none too quiet. Out of curiosity, he listened at Billy and Fred's door. It was perfectly quiet. Obviously the early hour was late for Tim and Jamie also, but Billy and Fred were fast asleep. Adam smiled to himself, peed, and returned to bed.

He and Evan had taken a long weekend at a gay resort in Key West. The place was a real eye opener for them. Clothing was optional and they couldn't help marvel at how so many men with ugly, obese bodies didn't mind baring themselves. On the other hand there was plenty of delicious eye candy as well. Through the thin walls, they could hear love making on both sides of them. The sounds aroused them. They lost track of how many noisy times they coupled that weekend, but they weren't counting. It never occurred to them that their noises were just as arousing to the couple on one side of them, and to the threesome on the other.

Adam smiled at the memory and strained to hear noises from Billy and Fred's room. He heard nothing.

Billy made a simple breakfast that morning, but he announced that they were all on vacation and would be eating their meals out from now on. That suited everyone just fine. After breakfast Fred drove them to Marina Del Rey where they had a light lunch on the pier. Fred urged them to save their appetites for dinner that night.

The air was refreshing and cool with very low humidity, and they ate outdoors. Late August in Florida meant very humid days and threats of hurricanes. Adam soaked in the glorious weather. The negative first impression of the very heavy traffic was giving way to impressions of a terrific climate and balmy days.

While they were enjoying lunch in the refreshing ocean air, Billy said casually, "We've invited a very dear friend of ours to join us at dinner tonight. He's a great guy." When he said that, he looked right at Adam and winked. Now what did that mean? Adam hoped it wasn't what he was thinking. Nobody would ever replace Evan. But even Adam had to admit to himself that a little bit of lustful, meaningless, unattached sex wouldn't be so bad for him. With that realization in his brain, Adam actually felt a pang of anticipation.

After lunch, Adam lost track of all the places Fred drove them to see. They never got out of the car, but Fred drove all over the Los Angeles area pointing out different sights. Adam recognized names that he had heard before, but that had no real meaning to him; Hollywood and Vine, Wilshire Boulevard, Sunset Boulevard, Santa Monica Boulevard, Beverly Hills, Rodeo Drive, the La Brea tar pits, Olivera Street (the old Mexican section of town), and many other places. It was really nice to see all the places he had read about and heard about. Some of the places he had seen in movies, but everything looked different in real life.

"I know you've heard of West Hollywood," Fred said. "It's a predominantly gay section. The restaurant we are going to tonight is there so you'll get to see West Hollywood this evening. But right now, we are going home to rest and freshen up."

Adam showered and decided to lie down for an hour or so before getting dressed for dinner. He lay down in bed in the very quiet guest room. He thought he heard a noise and he listened. The noise grew into many noises which got louder and louder. Now it was Billy and Fred who were going at it. It reminded Adam of just how noisy he remembered they were when they made love.

Billy brought Fred home to meet his folks right after graduation. The two young men came over to Adam and Evan for them to meet Fred. The four men made small talk for a while and then Billy looked very sheepish.

"Can I ask you guys for a favor?" he asked.

"Sure. Shoot." Evan said.

"Can we use your guest room for a little while? Fred and I are very noisy lovers and I am very inhibited in my folks' home."

Evan broke out laughing. "Sure," he said, "but I'll bet Adam and I are noisier. Take the bedroom at the head of the stairs."

It wasn't long before Adam and Evan were treated to shouts of, "Yeah, yeah, fuck me harder, fucker. You're holding back," and much much more. They might have gotten embarrassed but instead they became very horny and rushed up to their own bedroom. Afterward, the four of them laughed themselves silly at the language they had all used and heard.

Lying in his bed in Los Angeles so many years later, Adam fondly recalled the incident. Billy and Fred had been so handsome. He remembered thinking that if he didn't feel so fatherly toward the boys, he would have lusted after them. The noises from next door stopped and Adam dozed off.

He was roused from his nap by a knock on the door. He grabbed his robe and answered the door. Billy was standing there also wearing a robe.

"May I come in?" he asked. "I need to talk to you."

"Of course."

Billy entered and closed the door. The only place to sit was on the bed. He sat down and beckoned Adam to join him.

"Why do you look so serious?" Adam asked. "Is something wrong?"

"No, not really, but I have to tell you about something that happened a long time ago. It has bothered me almost all my life. I feel that if I don't confess it to you, I won't ever have any peace."

"I'm listening," Adam said.

"Promise not to hate me."

Adam put his arm around Billy and kissed him on the cheek. "I could never be angry with you, my son. I love you too much. I'm sure it's not half as bad as you think it is."

"It happened when I was sixteen. You were out this particular evening at your Spanish class and Evan was home alone."

The doorbell rang and Evan went to answer it. *Who the hell can it be*, he wondered. He opened the door and there stood Billy. The boy looked really scared.

"What's the matter?" Evan asked.

"Can I come in?"

"Of course." Billy came in and Evan shut the door.

"I need to speak to you," Billy said. "I'm really not afraid to talk to my dad about this, but before I do, I need some advice. Can we sit down somewhere comfortable?"

Evan waved his head toward the sofa, and the two of them sat down side by side. Billy's thigh was touching Evan's and Evan was very uncomfortable. He was a gay man and he knew that he shouldn't be alone with a minor boy. They looked at each other for a moment and finally Billy began to speak.

"Evan, I'm gay. I have a friend at school who wants to have sex with me, and I don't know what to do."

Evan was speechless. He never would have guessed. He put his arm around Billy and held him tight. "I can't help much," Evan said. "You have got to face it alone and deal with it alone. That doesn't mean that Adam and I aren't here for you. I just know your folks will support you too."

As Evan was comforting Billy, Billy had placed his hand on Evan's thigh and he was slowly inching up into territory reserved only for Adam. At first Evan didn't realize what was happening. All of his thoughts were on how he could help Billy come out.

Billy had almost reached Evan's crotch when Billy looked into Evan's eyes and began to kiss him. Billy's mouth on Evan's sent shudders through the older man's body. He knew he should pull away, but Billy had parted his lips and his tongue was probing Evan's. Finally Evan realized what was happening. He wanted desperately to pull away, but by now Billy was stroking his cock. Evan was hard and dripping pre-cum. Billy's seduction was successful and Evan was longing to make love to him.

"Teach me!" Billy begged. "Show me what to do. I want to have sex with my friend, but I want the first time to be with someone I love."

Billy told Evan he loved him. He knew he loved Billy. There was no way they could harm each other. Evan was over the top. He picked Billy up and carried him upstairs to his bedroom. Evan put Billy gently on his bed.

They were both skimpily dressed and undressing took just a moment. Evan took a moment to admire Billy's nubile young body. His cock was fully developed and almost as big as Adam's. Evan literally fell on top of Billy and devoured his rod in his mouth. Billy came gushing into Evan's mouth in a few short seconds. Evan swallowed every drop. He saved nothing for Billy.

"Please," Billy said, "I want to do that to you." Evan was not of a mind to stop him. He instructed Billy in the fine art of fellatio. Billy learned quickly and Evan came quickly. Following Evan's lead, he swallowed every drop also. Billy had never lost his erection and he realized that he was enjoying the hardest erection he had ever had in his life. It was so hard that it actually hurt him.

Evan took out some KY Jelly. He put some on Billy's finger and instructed him to grease his ass. He rolled on his back and Billy did as instructed.

"Now grease your dick and I think you can figure out what to do with it," Evan said. Billy entered Evan easily and started pumping. Evan thought that Billy felt so wonderful inside of him. Billy pumped harder and harder and came a second time. He kept himself inside of Evan until at last he softened and fell out.

Now the two lay facing each other, holding tight, rubbing their cocks together, and kissing passionately.

Finally Evan said, "Billy, Adam and I love you, but this must never happen again. I want you to go home now and nobody must ever know of this. Do you understand?"

Billy nodded. He was weeping.

"Someday you will come out to Adam and me, and I'll pretend to be shocked. Is that clear?" Billy nodded again. He dressed quickly and disappeared. They never coupled again.

Adam was speechless. He didn't know what to say. Billy was quiet now, trying to read Adam's face. What could Adam think or say? He had kept a secret from Evan and Evan had kept one from him. Adam had to wonder if Evan had ventured outside of their bed on other occasions, but he put the thought out of his head.

"Honest, Adam," Billy said. "It wasn't Evan's fault. It was easy for a young 16 year old to seduce an older man. It never happened again."

Finally Adam found his tongue. "Well," he said, "he sure put on an academy award performance when you came out to us."

"Please forgive me, Adam."

"There's nothing to forgive. It surely is water under the bridge." Adam put his arms around Billy and hugged him tightly. "Let's get ready for dinner," he said. "I'm anxious to check out West Hollywood and the blind date you have rounded up for me."

"Thank you Adam," Billy said. "You don't know how I have suffered keeping this secret. I feel a million percent better." He leaned into Adam and kissed him like a son would kiss a father. Then he left the room.

Why Evan, you old reprobate, Adam thought. *Well don't sweat it old man, wherever you are. I still love you, and I always will. Even if you slept with a hundred different men, nothing could change how I feel about you.*

Adam looked up to heaven and smiled. Suddenly his smile turned to dread. He distinctly heard Evan's voice. He did not imagine it. "Don't live like a hermit, big guy. Get out in the world and enjoy yourself. Take a lover. Live until you die. It's my parting wish for you."

The voice disappeared and Adam composed himself.

You old fart, he thought. *I'll bet you did sleep with a lot of guys and now you're feeling guilty so you want me to do the same. Well, I won't assuage your guilt. I'm a single man and I can sleep with anyone I want to, and I won't feel guilty.* On reflection, he added. *It doesn't mean I don't still love you, you old coot.*

CHAPTER EIGHT

This time when they entered the restaurant they were immediately taken to a table. As soon as they were seated, the twinkie waiter handed them menus. Fred informed him that they were waiting for one more guest to join them. Having said that, his cell phone rang. "Jim. Where are you?" he asked. He listened a few minutes, said "OK," and closed his phone.

"Jim's stuck in traffic on the 101, but he should be here in about 15 minutes. Let's have a drink." He waved to the young waiter who came running. They all ordered a cocktail. Fred made a toast to their friendship and everyone took a sip. Adam turned to Billy.

"OK sonny," he said, "tell me about this Jim. I saw you wink at me when you mentioned him so what's going on."

"Fred and I met Jim on a gay cruise," Billy began. "He and his partner, Blake, were seated at our dinner table. We hit it off right away, especially since we were all from Los Angeles. We became good friends and continued to be good friends after the trip ended. Blake was 10 years older than Fred and I. He died last year of colon cancer. Jim is 75, eight years older than we. They were together for 45 years."

"You wouldn't be trying to fix up two old widowers, would you?" Adam asked.

"Why not? You'll only be here for 9 or so days. Why not have someone about your own age to hang with and to go out with us? I have Fred, and Jamie and Tim have each other. We'll have more fun coupled. Besides all that sensible stuff, I want to make your visit here so memorable, you'll want to come back."

Adam could hear Evan's voice telling him to have fun.

"How does Jim feel about your matchmaking efforts?" Adam wanted to know.

"I told him that I had visitors from Florida and that I wanted him to meet them. That's all."

"Them?"

Billy nodded sheepishly. "After all there are three of you visiting here. Jim thought it was a great idea. He used to live in Florida, but moved here many years ago. He and his partner were gay bashed in Miami about forty years ago. They moved here hoping to find a friendlier place to live. He's anxious to meet some of his old country men."

"I've been acting negatively," Adam said, "but actually I am looking forward to meeting him." Adam was almost finished with his cocktail when Jim Madison came rushing in.

"So sorry to be late," he said. "I left plenty of time for traffic delays, but you can never know when an accident will tie things up even worse." Fred made introductions all around and Adam felt that Jim held his hand a bit too long. He didn't mind at all. The seat on Adam's right had purposely been left open for Jim. He sat down and Adam studied him carefully.

He was no more than 5 feet 7 inches tall, and a smidgeon overweight. Adam had never admitted it to Evan, but he was attracted to slightly overweight men. He longed to hold their love handles while fucking them. The reason he never told Evan about his secret desire was that Evan never carried an extra pound during his whole life. Jim had a full head of wavy silver hair. Adam found that particularly attractive. His eyes were a pale blue and when he smiled they crinkled up. His face was still boyish. Adam did not feel guilty at all that he found Jim very attractive. He could not help but wonder what Jim was thinking about him.

The waiter interrupted his thoughts to take their orders. When he left the table, Jim said to Adam, "I know it's very unlikely, but I have the strongest feeling that we have met before. It would have to have been over forty years ago when I lived in Florida. I'll think about it."

The conversation during dinner was light and airy. Adam found out that Fred and Billy intended to take them all to Venice Beach the next day and Jim was coming along. When Adam heard that, a feeling came over him that he couldn't identify. For sure, it was a feeling he hadn't felt in many, many years.

Suddenly Jim screamed out, "AHA! I remember where I met you before. I think you were in my night school Spanish class."

(*I think you are in my English Lit class, Evan said.*)

"How could you possibly remember that?" Adam asked in amazement. "Anyway, you aren't familiar to me at all."

Jim removed his wallet and took out a picture. "Here's a picture of Blake and me taken when I was in that class. Maybe it will jar your memory."

Adam looked at the picture and started to laugh.

"Yes, of course. I must admit I had the hots for you, but I was in a loving and committed relationship and would never have acted on it. Besides, I assumed that you were straight," Adam said.

Billy was seated on the other side of Adam. He leaned over and whispered in Adam's ear, "Too bad. You two could have had fun, while Evan and I were going at it."

"Very funny," Adam whispered back.

"Yeah," Jim said. "I thought you were hot also, and I assumed you were straight."

"It's never too late to pick up where you left off," Tim said, and Jim and Adam both blushed a deep red.

"I never finished the course," Jim said. "Blake and I were bashed and beat up pretty badly before the end of the semester. I never went back and shortly thereafter we moved to LA."

"Sorry," Adam said, "but I guess I didn't notice you well enough after all. I simply don't recall paying any attention to the fact that you dropped out."

After dinner, they all went to the bar area. There were tables of two and four. Adam and Jim took a table for two and the others sat next to them at a table for four. A waiter took their drink orders. Jim had a coke because he was driving and so did Fred. After they were served, Jim asked, "How long has it been since your partner died?"

"It'll be four months in a few days. Billy told me it's a year for you."

"Nearly," Jim said, "it's been tough. I began dating a few months after Blake died. I've even had sex, but nothing special. I don't like being alone. I know it can never be the same passionate love that Blake and I shared, but I would welcome finding someone to share my remaining days."

"I am not presuming you have me in mind," Adam said, "but I am curious. Blake was three years older than you and he's gone. I'm eight years older than you. Would that color your thinking?"

"I don't think so, especially not with you. We are still not presuming you understand, but you look healthier and younger than I do," Jim complimented Adam.

"Thank you," Adam smiled. "I think you still look like a kid."

"Can you still….?" Jim left the sentence hanging in the air.

"Well, Evan and I had oral sex the evening before he died. He was 88 and he had no trouble reaching a climax. For that matter neither did I. Anal sex had been out for many years. Neither of us got hard enough anymore to penetrate. Viagra and the other stuff just didn't work for either of us. Since he died, I answer nature's call whenever necessary with the palm of my hand."

"It was pretty much the same with Blake and me, except that he was so sick at the end, we hadn't had sex for over a year before he died."

Adam noticed a tear in Jim's eye so he laid his hand on top of Jim's. The two men looked at each other and smiled. Jim took Adam's hand in both of his, raised it to his lips, and kissed the back of Adam's hand. With his other hand Adam stroked Jim's teary cheek.

"This time I am going to be presumptuous," Jim said. "Why don't you come home with me and we can meet the others at the beach tomorrow?"

Adam laughed. "I've got a better idea. There is no way I could fit into one of your bathing suits, but one of Tim's would fit you perfectly. Why don't you come home with me? That is, if you can tolerate the sounds of love making from every room in the house."

"That sounds like a plan," Jim said with a big grin on his face. "As for the sounds of passion, I used to go to the baths a lot when I was young and single, and I grew used to it. It turns you on actually. Let's clear it with Billy and Fred."

At the other table Billy began to laugh. "Are you kidding," he asked. "I've been listening to every word you two have said and it is more than OK with us. I've been playing Cupid and I shot an arrow into the air, and it landed exactly where I wanted it to."

"Sonny, you and I are going to have words," Adam mocked.

Suddenly all six of them had a burning desire to go home. Adam rode home with Jim. They both felt a little awkward and there was little conversation. Finally at a red light, Jim put his hand on Adam's thigh and Adam returned the favor. That sort of broke the ice.

Jamie and Tim used the guest bathroom first, then Jim. Billy supplied him with a new toothbrush and a disposable razor. Adam took up the rear. When he returned to his room, the bedside light was on and the overhead light had been turned off. Jim was lying on top of the covers. He was naked and bade Adam to join him. Adam had put on a pair of underwear which he quickly discarded. When Jim saw Adam's massive cock, he involuntarily shouted out, "Wow, I hope you won't be disappointed when you see my little one."

Adam looked at Jim's nakedness. He had an average size cock and Adam said, "You look just fine to me." He lay down next to Jim and the two men shared their first kiss together. It was a rather chaste kiss, but the second and third kisses became more urgent. At last their tongues met. Adam nearly swooned. It had been so long and it felt so good. He started to say, *Evan I love you so much,* but stopped himself just in time. Instead, he said, "Oh Jim, it has been so long and this feels so good."

Suddenly Jim disengaged himself and slithered down Adam's body. At the first touch of Jim's tongue on his cock, Adam could feel himself getting hard. He knew it wouldn't be a solid ram rod like in the olden days, but he knew that it would beat anything he had experienced in the past few years. He wondered how hard Jim would get.

It didn't happen quickly, but Adam began to feel the erotic signs of an approaching orgasm. He stopped Jim from his labors. "Not yet," he said. "I want this to last all night."

"Yes, yes," Jim whispered. He crept up the bed until his lips met Adam's. They kissed and stroked each other's cocks until Adam began to move down Jim's body. He took Jim's cock into his mouth.

The difference in size between Jim and Evan was hardly noticeable. Adam devoured Jim's semi erect cock as though he hadn't eaten in months, and that was nearly the truth. He grabbed Jim's love handles as he had always dreamed of doing and went at it so fervently, that Jim lost the restraint that Adam had shown and began to cum generously into Adam's mouth. Adam swallowed everything greedily. He used to save some to give back to Evan, but there was nothing left for Jim.

"I'm sorry," he said. "I didn't save any for you."

Jim laughed and said. "I don't want to save any for you either. This time don't hold back." He went down on Adam, who came after a few minutes screaming loudly. The scream was heard by the other four inhabitants of the house. They all smiled and thanked God for Adam and Jim's good fortune.

Adam and Jim fell asleep on top of the covers. They were naked. In the middle of the night something disturbed Adam's sleep. He opened his eyes to find the room bathed in an eerie glow. Evan was leaning over him and kissing him. It wasn't the Evan who died an old man. It was Evan in his twenties, looking exactly as he did on the day he picked Adam up at The Male Room. It was a naked Evan.

On the other side of the room another apparition was leaning over Jim and kissing him. The apparition appeared to be about thirty. Adam could tell that he had black hair. His body was about the same height and weight as Jim's. He too was naked. The apparition stopped kissing Jim and looked at Adam. He smiled and walked over (or rather floated) to Evan. The two ghosts took each other's hands and disappeared. The room grew dark and Adam fell asleep again.

In the morning he asked Jim if he could see the picture in his wallet again, the one of him and Blake. There was no doubt, the two visitors last night were Evan and Blake. They had given Adam and Jim their blessings. Adam didn't know for sure if it was real, wishful thinking, or a simple dream, but he told Jim about it.

"I believe it was real," Jim said. "I dreamed last night that Blake came to me and repeatedly kissed me on the lips. It was like he was saying that he was so pleased for me, for both of us."

"Oh Jim," Adam cried. "I so want to believe that."

He distinctly heard Evan say, "Believe it."

CHAPTER NINE

For the next few days Jim and Adam lived in a dream world. They acted like two young lovers who had their whole lives ahead of them. Then reality set in. They lived three thousand miles apart.

They began to analyze their situations. Adam lived in an independent living facility. He had no real friends there except Jamie, and Jamie had moved out the day before the flight to California. If he moved to LA, the only real friends he would leave behind were Jamie and Tim. But in Los Angeles he would have Billy and Fred. Real family. Of course, he would also have Jim.

Jim lived in his own private home. He had lived in LA for four decades. He had an army of friends including Billy and Fred. The choice seemed obvious, but Adam didn't know how to tell Jamie. As it turned out he didn't have to. All six of them were spending a quiet afternoon at Billy and Fred's backyard pool. Fred, Jim and Tim were dozing on lounge chairs soaking up the sun. Billy was getting the barbeque ready. He decided to make a backyard dinner party that evening.

Jamie asked Adam if he could have a word with him. He took Adam's hand and led him into the house.

"You look very serious," Adam said.

"I am," Jamie answered. "I want you to listen to me carefully. None of us are blind here. We can all see how things are going with you and Jim. Even if you don't know it, this thing with you two is more than buddy fucking. We can all see real love." Adam started to open his mouth, but Jamie stopped him.

"I know that nobody will ever replace Evan in your heart, and that's OK. I can tell you that nobody will ever replace Blake in Jim's heart. That doesn't mean that the two of you can't find happiness together. Now I guess you are going to tell me that you two have been discussing the possibility of one of you moving."

Adam smiled. "Jamie, my friend," he said, "you are so wise. We have discussed it at length, and the conclusion is obvious that it is I who should move. I just didn't know how to tell you. The only negative in the mix is moving away from you and Tim."

Jamie took Adam's hands and held them in his own. "We can all afford to fly back and forth from coast to coast once a year," he said. "We'll come for a visit about this time of year every year. Isn't the weather to die for? We can stay until we wear out our welcome. And you and Jim can come in the winter for as long as you want. We'll be together old chum. How does that sound?"

Adam took Jamie in his arms and embraced him warmly. Since Jamie had tied up with Tim, they had dispensed with manly hugs. They held each other tightly. Each could feel the other's package. "I love you," Adam said. "I'll miss you a lot. You better not default on your telephone bill because you can expect a lot of calls from me."

They went back to the pool area and Adam went immediately to Jim. He whispered something in his ear and Jim jumped up quickly. The two embraced and kissed passionately.

"Listen up everyone," Adam yelled. "I'm moving to Los Angeles and I'll be living with Jim. I've cleared it with Jamie and we are both cool with it." The announcement was followed by a six way group hug. Billy was sobbing like a baby. "Oh Fred darling," he said. "We'll have family here at last."

After everyone calmed down, Billy said that he was sorry they were having an informal barbeque that evening because this called for a major celebration.

"Not a problem," Jamie said. "On our last night out, let's dine at some fancy restaurant and make the love birds an engagement party. But hear this. The party is on Tim and me so you can bloody well leave your 'effing' wallets at home, and I don't want to hear any objections."

They continued to swim and lounge alternately until about 4:30 PM. Then Billy asked everyone to go upstairs to freshen up, and to get back to the pool area for the barbeque at about six. As had become habit, Jamie and Tim used the guest bathroom first. While they were in there, Jim and Adam engaged themselves in a lusty game of sixty-nine. Neither of them came, and it didn't bother them in the least. Just to be intimate once again, with a man they loved, was reward enough.

On the flight home, Adam gave up his seat to Tim so he could sit with Jamie. He took Tim's odd seat, which was just behind Jamie's. Once airborne, Adam began to make a list of all the things he had to do prior to leaving. Since the monthly fee at The Sunnydale House included everything except telephone, there was little for Adam to discontinue. He needed to give thirty days notice, and so he would have to pay for the month of October and be out by October 31. He hoped to be out long before that.

He began to doze off.

————————

Evan and he had been out to dinner for Evan's sixtieth birthday. Adam had big bed plans for Evan when they got home. He intended on giving Evan a *rousing* birthday present. They got ready for bed as usual and began to cuddle as usual. Adam got hard the minute Evan fondled him, but Evan remained soft. Adam had noticed that recently Evan wasn't responding as usual, and that he seemed to want sex less and less. In fact, if Adam wanted to face facts, Evan seemed to actually be avoiding sex. His libido had descended into the cellar.

Adam did everything he knew which would ordinarily arouse Evan, but he had no success and Evan remained flaccid. Finally they both gave up trying, but Adam was left with a throbbing hard-on and he begged Evan to do something about it. Evan said that he really didn't feel like it and he rolled over and faced away from Adam. Now his libido seemed to have gone down to the sub-basement.

Adam feared, and rightly so, that it might be something physical and he begged Evan to see a urologist. Evan poo poohed and refused to go. Finally one day he spotted a trace of blood in his urine and he made an appointment with the doctor.

Evan was diagnosed with prostate cancer and treatment was begun immediately. Standard radiation and seeding treatments failed to make a difference, and in the end Evan had to have his prostate surgically removed.

During the time Evan was indisposed, he told Adam that he really wouldn't mind if Adam wanted to have sex with other men. Adam told him to shut up because it wasn't going to happen.

"Then promise me," Evan told Adam, "if anything happens to me, you'll find someone else to be with. I can't bear to think of you as a lonely old man."

It took Evan six months of aftercare treatment before he began to desire sex again. The doctor told him that the operation went well, and that in time he would have full sexual pleasure. There was only one thing that would be different. His orgasms would not produce ejaculation. He would feel all the right sensations and emotions, but he would not spew out semen. The semen would be ejected from his body in his urine.

The first time they were able to make love after surgery, Evan was truly a tiger. He was as excited as Adam. He came quickly in Adam's mouth, but Adam missed the warm tangy feeling of Evan's cum shooting into his mouth. He could not let Evan know that, and so he declared triumphantly, "This is great. I get all the pleasure and none of the mess." As for Evan, he was grateful that he could orgasm, and that it was actually more pleasurable than before. He attributed that to being cancer free.

———————————

Adam slept long and well. He was awakened by the flight attendant, who told him that they were beginning their descent into Ft. Lauderdale. Upon awakening, Adam remembered Evan's wish that he should find someone else if he should pass before Adam. A warm feeling came over Adam, and he knew that his union with Jim was blessed by Evan.

The next couple of weeks were very busy for Adam. The furniture in his apartment belonged to the facility, but he had to pack his personal belongings. He and Evan had intermingled all their clothes, and there were no articles of clothing that belonged strictly to either one of them. As a result, Adam had given nothing to charity when Evan died. He probably had too much clothing, but didn't know what he would need in California. He concluded that Jim could help him decide at the other end. Consequently, he had twelve full boxes of clothing. Picture albums and other personal household accessories accounted for three more boxes. The only things that Adam did not pack were the things that he thought he would need for his trip to California, including the two suitcases in the closet.

Three days before his departure, the shipping company came and picked up his stuff. He figured that it should arrive about the same time as he did. Since leaving California, he and Jim called each other at least twice a day in spite of the time difference. As the days dwindled down, they got more and more excited. They were as giddy and anticipatory as two high school kids.

The night before departure, Tim and Jamie took Adam out for a farewell dinner at a five star restaurant. The evening would have been more pleasant if Jamie hadn't started crying several times during the dinner. In spite of the fact that Jim and Adam promised to come back east in February, Jamie could not control his tears. He not only kept giving Adam all the credit for his having met Tim, an event which totally changed his life, but he kept saying how much he would miss Adam. There was nothing Tim or Adam could do so they just let him cry it out. Tim and Jamie wanted to take Adam to the airport in the morning, but his flight was so early, he wouldn't let them. He arranged for a cab instead.

———————

It was 3:00 PM on a Sunday evening. The cab pulled up their driveway and the driver honked the horn. Evan grabbed his suitcase, gave Adam a quickie kiss and left. He was going to New York for a week on business.

When he was comfortably seated in his window seat in the first class cabin, a handsome man of about fifty sat down next to him. They smiled at each other and when the man got seated, he extended his hand to Adam and said, "Hi, I'm Mark Allen, with Consolidated Bakeries. I'm headed for New York for the week on business. I'll be returning Friday evening on the 5:30. How about you?"

"Evan Morrisey's the name, and same, same. I'll be in New York for the week on business also. I'm with World Wide Electronics. I think we'll be on the same return flight. Where are you staying?"

"At The Hilton on Seventh Avenue. How about you?"

Evan laughed. "At the Hilton," he said. "Wanna share a cab from the airport?"

"It'll be a pleasure, Evan," Mark said.

An exceptionally handsome male flight attendant leaned over them and asked what he could serve them to drink prior to take off. Evan's groin stirred looking at the young man, and he did not misread the look on Mark's face either. From the way he looked at the flight attendant, Evan was sure that Mark was gay and he intended to find out. All through the flight, the attendant paid special attention to Mark and Evan.

Evan ordered a whiskey sour. He had to wonder why? He never drank whiskey sours. Then it came to him. That was the first drink he ever bought for Adam at the Male Room. He tried to attach some significance to that, but nothing came to mind. Mark ordered a scotch and soda.

During the flight, Evan ascertained through casual conversation that Mark was a long time Ft. Lauderdale resident. "Where are your favorite places to go in Ft. Lauderdale?" Evan asked.

"Well, I love the theater, but I'm very much a homebody. I rarely go to clubs or bars."

"Same here," Evan commented. "If I do go to a club I like to visit 'Dorothy's House.'" Dorothy's House was a well-known gay bar. Evan figured that if Mark was straight, the name would mean nothing to him. If he was gay, he would surely know the place.

Mark smiled. At the same time he placed his hand on Evan's knee. Evan was mad at himself. He should have been angry at Mark's boldness, but he liked the feel and wanted to return the favor.

"If we have something to celebrate," Mark said, "that's the place my partner and I are apt to go to celebrate."

"Wow," Evan offered. "That's where Adam and I go also. What's your partner's name?"

"Cole," Mark said simply and moved his hand slightly higher up Evan's thigh.

Evan's emotions were totally conflicted. He knew that he and Mark could have a cool week of sex in New York without either of their partners ever knowing. But would it be right? Right or wrong didn't seem very important when you were facing a week of abstinence in a swinging town like New York. Evan placed his hand on Mark's knee, encouraging him. When the handsome flight attendant passed by, they made no attempt to retreat. It was obvious to both of them that the young man was gay and he was flirting with both of them.

Early in the flight, Mark asked for a blanket for him and Evan. They both covered themselves and now they were able to fondle each other under their blankets. Mark actually took his cock out of his trousers so Evan did the same. They stroked each other and smiled at each other, but wisely stopped before either of them could cum.

When Sean, the flight attendant began to serve dinner, they got themselves decent again. "I think it's going to be one hell of a week," Mark said.

"I couldn't agree more," Evan concluded. He tried to feel guilt, but all he felt was that he was getting hornier and hornier.

At the end of the trip, the flight attendant gave each of them a card and said that he would be in New York for three nights if either of them wanted to call him.

They shared a cab to the hotel. At the hotel they asked if they could get two rooms close by.

"I have two adjoining rooms," the desk clerk said. "There is a door between them."

"Perfect," they both said in unison. One bellhop took them both to their rooms.

Mark went into his room and Evan went into his. They both locked the outside door and opened the adjoining door.

"I'm going to shower and freshen up," Mark said.

"Me too," Evan agreed.

"Why don't you shower with me?" Mark asked.

"Capital idea!" Evan said. He undressed rapidly and grabbed a towel from the bathroom. He retrieved his toiletry kit from his carry on case. It was the same one he had used in the army. He literally ran into Mark's room. Mark was already in the bathroom adjusting the water temperature in the shower. Evan deposited his stuff on the vanity and came up behind Mark, jabbing him in the ass with his hardened rod. Mark turned around. The two men embraced and began to kiss passionately. Adam was out of sight and out of mind. Apparently Cole was out of mind also.

In the shower they sucked each other off alternately. Mark's technique was different than Adam's and Evan enjoyed the subtle differences. When they were out of the shower and drying themselves, they discussed it, and Mark felt exactly as Evan did. The minor differences added to their enjoyment.

They dressed and went down to the bar for a drink. There they discussed inviting Sean, the flight attendant, to their love nest the next evening. Both agreed that it would be fun and Mark volunteered to call him. Before retiring they made up to meet for breakfast.

They had breakfast together and when Mark called Sean, he invited him to join them for dinner. Sean was more than enthusiastic and he met them at a restaurant on Restaurant Row. The three of them acted rather childishly and kept feeling each other up under the table.

Sean suggested that before retiring for a night of pleasure they should all go to Greenwich Village for a nightcap.

"Is The Male Room still in business?" Evan asked.

"I never heard of it," Sean said. "Where is it located?"

Evan had to really search his memory to remember at what cross streets the bar had been located.

"There's a gay bar there now called The Pickle Barrel. It's not a bad place. We can go there, and if we don't like it we can always leave."

The Pickle Barrel was very little changed from the way Evan remembered The Male Room from more than twenty years ago. A poster in the lobby announced that Mother Eve would entertain this coming Saturday night. Evan was glad he would be home by then. Eve's picture was the same one that had been in the lobby when Evan had met him. Under all his drag make up, he might actually get away with it. The biggest change was the music. No longer was the music soft and sensual so that bodies could rub together, it was blaring rock and roll music. Evan and Mark winced when they entered but Sean started gyrating his hips.

"Come on," he said to Evan as he dragged him on to the dance floor. Evan lasted half a dance because he was huffing and puffing so hard, so Mark finished the dance with Sean. They both told the young man to find another partner to dance with, but they assured him that they both had the stuff to make him happy in bed.

For some reason they couldn't fathom, Evan's room had two queen size beds and Mark's had one king size bed. They decided to use Mark's room. The three men undressed and all three squeezed into the shower. It was too crowded to do anything, but by the time they came out of the shower each of them had a raging erection.

Mark and Evan lay Sean between them, and each proceeded to tongue every part of Sean's body that they could reach. They sucked his cock and balls more than any other body part. Sean writhed and moaned in ecstasy. Then they turned him over and explored his backside. They both rimmed him generously. Both of the older men were convinced that youth did indeed have its day. Licking a young firm body was a thing of the past for them. Both of them were making love to middle aged men, and now they could tell the difference. It was a nice diversion.

They turned him over again and went to work on his cock. When Sean started to cum they both tried to swallow as much of his spunk as they could. Evan had forgotten just how much spunk a young man could produce. After he recovered a bit, Sean asked his two older lovers to please fuck him. Mark took condoms and lube from his suitcase and they all got ready. Sean lay on his back. He placed a pillow under his butt and raised his legs. Evan went in first, but refrained from cumming. He pulled out and gave Mark an opportunity. They went back and forth like this for as long as they could. Sean was happy at how long they took to cum. After about the fifth entry, Evan could not hold back. Mark allowed himself to cum after Evan did.

The older men thought that Sean would spend the night with them, but he said he had an early flight to Buffalo and a return to New York in the afternoon so he really had to leave. When they called his hotel the next evening they were informed that he had checked out.

"No doubt he is spending the night with some rich geezer who can be his sugar daddy." Mark surmised.

Evan and Mark spent every night in New York making love. They did take in some shows, but that was the only entertainment they cared to partake in. They preferred their fucking bed, as Mark so crudely put it.

They promised to get together with Adam and Cole at home, but when they parted at the airport, they never saw each other again. Both thought it would be wise not to get together ever again.

Adam was at the airport to pick Evan up. At the luggage carousel, Mark and Evan shook hands when they said goodbye.

"Who was that?" Adam asked.

"Just another guy travelling on business. We happened to sit next to each other going and coming."

CHAPTER TEN

The day was finally here. The cab dropped Adam off at curbside. And he checked in his two suitcases. He had a carry on and proceeded to security. After the usual searches he was allowed into the departure terminal. He had the first flight out this morning and erroneously assumed that the plane would leave on time, but according to the monitor it would be leaving a half hour later than scheduled. Adam's impatience knew no bounds. He bought a newspaper and sat down in the waiting area until he could board the plane. He wasn't used to getting up at such an early hour and he began to doze off.

Adam was waiting for Evan at the baggage terminal. His flight from New York was a half hour late. Finally the passengers from Evan's flight started to approach the carousel, which had not yet started to turn. Adam spotted Evan, but he didn't approach him because he was deep in conversation with another passenger. There was a look going back and forth between them, that was unmistakable. Adam instinctively knew that Evan had been intimate with this man. He had to examine his feelings. He had no proof, but what disturbed him was the fact that it didn't really bother him. He knew that Evan loved him. He came home to their house and their bed, and that was all that mattered.

The two men retrieved their baggage and shook hands. Only then did Adam approach Evan.

"Who was that?" Adam asked.

"Just another guy travelling on business. We happened to sit next to each other going and coming."

"That's good," Adam said. "A good travelling companion always makes the flight go faster."

"You're right, honey," Evan said. "It did. Now let's get home so I can make up for lost time."

When they exited the terminal to walk to the parking ramp, Evan saw Mark standing at curbside. A car pulled up and a young man, a very young man, got out. He bore a strong resemblance to Mark. He embraced Mark and helped him put his luggage in the trunk. The young man was even younger than Sean. As the two men were getting into the car, Evan distinctly heard the young man ask, "Did you have a successful trip, Dad?"

Fuck! Mark was a married man. He had himself a fling. Evan wondered how many other "straight" men were out there yearning to live as their true selves, a gay man. For a second, Evan was angry at Mark, but then he felt sorry for him. He must be racked with guilt, shame and sexual frustration.

"Did you have a successful trip, Dad?" Adam heard those words as clearly as Evan, and wanted to kick himself for thinking that Evan and this guy could have been intimate.

The squawk box roused Adam. His flight was ready for boarding. Adam kept thinking that in about five and a half hours, he would be starting a new phase in his life. It would probably be the shortest, but he was determined to make the most of it. As soon as they were in the air, Adam's mind wandered off to another happy plane trip.

Evan retired two years before Adam. They had agreed that when Adam retired they would do a grand tour of Europe. They had never been abroad before as civilians, and they decided not to do it on their own as so many of their friends had. They searched the travel brochures until they found a twenty-one day guided tour of Europe. The tour included all the major cities they wanted to see: Dublin, London, Paris, Brussels, Amsterdam, Vienna, Rome, Florence, Venice, and Salerno. Besides wishing to see these places as other tourists, they obtained gay guides to these cities, and planned on including gay activities whenever the tour itinerary read, 'free time.'

They had to fly to JFK Airport in New York to meet the rest of the group and they were to fly to Europe on Aer Lingus with their other travelling companions. Evan and Adam were so excited when they told Hans and Barry that they actually hyperventilated. They expected their friends to be excited for them, but they were met with stony silence instead.

"What?" Evan asked.

"How could you not have asked us if we would want to do the trip with you?" Barry asked, sounding very hurt.

Evan was stunned. They hadn't even thought about asking Barry and Hans.

"But you are both still working. We didn't think you could get away," Evan lied.

"We both have plenty of vacation time, and we would have been delighted to make the trip with you. Didn't you want us along?"

"Are you kidding? That would be fantastic," Adam shouted. "There's plenty of time to book you on our tour. Let's call the travel agent the first thing in the morning."

Two months later they were waiting to board the plane for New York at the airport in Ft. Lauderdale. They had decided to spend two days in New York before meeting their group at JFK for the flight to Europe. Their mood was light and jovial. They were all full of great expectations for the trip. They had obtained theater tickets for two of the biggest musical hits on Broadway, and they booked two adjoining rooms at one of New York's finest hotels. They agreed that money was no object on this trip, because it was probably the only overseas trip they would ever make.

They arrived in New York at 11 AM, and took a cab to the hotel. They barely got into the vehicle with all their luggage. Once they got into their rooms they opened the adjoining door between them. It remained open for the two nights that they occupied the room. Evan thought about his week with Mark, but quickly wiped the memory away.

They decided to have lunch in Greenwich Village. Adam and Evan wanted to revisit the NYU campus to see how much it had changed, and they wanted to see how much The Village had changed as well. They went to The Village first and had lunch at a neat looking luncheonette. The area was much more congested than they remembered it, and it had grown a wee bit seedy. Evan pointed out to Adam that The Male Room had changed it's name to The Pickle Barrel, as if it was a great surprise to him. "Probably it has a new owner," he remarked. The campus remained relatively unchanged.

"After the show tonight, let's come back to The Village for a nightcap before going to bed. God knows we don't have to get up early," Hans suggested. They all agreed.

They took a cab back to the hotel intending to shower and shave before dinner. Adam made reservations at the same restaurant that he and Mark had eaten at years before. It was in the theater district and they wouldn't have to rush dinner. They had plenty of time and when they got to their rooms, Adam announced that he was going to take a short nap. The four of them had often gone together to the nude gay beach in Ft. Lauderdale. There was no modesty between them, so when Adam announced that he was going to take a nap, he undressed completely and plopped down on the bed in one of the rooms. He wasn't sure whose room it was.

"That's a great idea," Barry said. He undressed and plopped down beside Adam. The two snuggled together. Hans and Evan thought nothing of it.

"We might as well nap too," Evan said, and he and Hans went into the other room, got naked and lay down together.

Big mistake!!!

Two horny, naked gay men lying together can mean only one thing. Before they realized what was happening, Adam and Barry were cuddling, fondling and stroking their cocks. The mismatched couple was only doing what comes naturally. In the other room Evan and Hans were doing the same thing.

Eventually Barry whispered to Adam, "It's been so long since I nibbled on foreskin." He slid right down and started to tongue Adam's cock, nipping delicately at his foreskin. For a fleeting moment, Adam realized this was wrong. He wanted to stop Barry, but he was too far gone. He came, gushing into Barry's mouth. His screams were more than noticed in the other room, where Evan was sucking Hans's cock.

There was no stopping either couple now, and they made passionate love to each other for over an hour. Totally spent, both couples lay back, and the immensity of what had just happened began to sink in.

"Come with me," Evan said to Hans. He took Hans's hand and led him into the other room. Adam and Barry were lying side by side, holding hands. They were both crying.

"Why are you crying?" Hans asked.

"We got carried away. We should never have done what we did."

"Nonsense," Evan said. "What we did is the most natural thing in the world. We love each other so why not show that love physically?"

He turned to Hans and then to Barry in the bed and said, "Hans and Barry, I love you both unconditionally, and I want to make love to both of you whenever the mood and opportunity arises. You are each a big part of my life and please don't exclude yourselves because I sure don't want to exclude you."

There was silence. Adam didn't know what to make of it. Finally Hans broke the silence. "You are right, Evan," he said. "We are soul mates, we four, and we should share our bodies as well as our souls. I love you all so much, with all my heart and soul. I almost died in the camps and you are all God's gifts to me."

Adam and Barry leapt out of bed. The four of them kissed and embraced each other and pressed their now limp cocks together.

"This is going to be one hell of a vacation," Hans said.

The big jet landed late in the morning at LAX. The flight attendant admonished the passengers to stay seated with seat belts tightened until they were safely stopped at the terminal. Adam could barely contain himself. While they were taxiing the tarmac, they were allowed to use their cell phones. Adam called Jim. "We're on the ground," he said. "It's taking this monster forever to get to the terminal."

"I'm at the baggage carousel," Jim said. "Look for me there. By the way your cartons arrived late yesterday. I took the liberty of opening the ones marked 'clothing' and I hung everything up. I hope you don't mind. I left the cartons marked 'personal' for you to open."

"Of course I don't mind. I wasn't exactly looking forward to the job. Thanks for doing it for me. See you in a bit."

Jim carried one suitcase, and Adam carried the other and his carry on, to Jim's car. Once seated in the car, Jim leaned over and kissed Adam before they put on their seat belts.

"At the risk of sounding like a dirty old man," Jim said, "as soon as we get home let's shower together and hop right into bed."

"You get no argument from me," Adam laughed.

The shower felt really good to Adam. His bones ached from the long plane ride and the cascading warm waters relieved him. The two old men fondled and played, but it was difficult for them to kneel down on the tile floor to service each other. As soon as they were dried off they fell into bed. Their arms wrapped around each other. Their cocks ground together. They kissed and kissed and ground and ground until Adam could stand it no longer. He slithered down Jim's body and grabbed his cock, stroking it gently. Then he began licking up and down the underside of Jim's shaft. Jim grew a slight bit harder. Adam put Jim's cock in his mouth, and his tongue kept licking Jim's shaft. Every so often he nibbled Jim's foreskin as he remembered the pleasure Barry had given him.

It took a few moments, but Jim began to moan. His buttocks began to rise and fall as he tried to thrust harder into Adam's mouth. When he came, it revived old memories for Adam, memories which had faded after Evan's prostate operation. Difficult as it was, Adam refrained from swallowing. Instead he pulled himself up and kissed Jim, passing him his own spunk. Jim swallowed greedily and whispered to Adam. I need a couple of minutes to breathe again and then it will be my turn.

"While you are recuperating," Adam said, "turn over." Jim rolled over on his belly and Adam proceeded to rim him. Jim gave out one long sigh of pleasure.

"Nice, nice," he repeated over and over. Finally he said, "It's my turn."

In spite of Adam being older than Jim, Jim's expertise at fallatio helped Adam achieve orgasm very quickly. Jim was disappointed and he jokingly told Adam so. He wanted to keep Adam in his mouth for hours.

"Next time, love," was all Adam could say while trying to catch his breath.

They lay side by side, cuddling and kissing and they both dozed off. When they awoke it was mid afternoon. They showered again, separately, and went downstairs to the kitchen for a light bite.

"Is there anything special you would like to do this afternoon?" Jim asked.

"Yes. I'd like to be with you."

"No problem. By the way, we are picking Billy up tonight for dinner. He can't wait to see you and he wants to treat us to dinner as a welcoming present."

"I suppose that Fred is in Sacramento. Poor Billy. I wouldn't blame him if he had someone on the side," Adam said.

"Don't be too shocked," Jim said, "but Fred has a fuck buddy in Sacramento and Billy has one here. They gave each other mutual consent. I don't think it diminishes the love they have one iota. It seems, in fact, to strengthen their love."

"Like I said, I wouldn't blame them."

"Didn't you and Evan ever have a third party in bed with you, or maybe even cheat on each other? I know Blake and I did. It might have bothered some people, but I didn't mind. Fucking and loving are two very different verbs," Jim noted.

"The answer to your question is yes," Adam said. "The first evening we spend alone together remind me to tell you about Hans and Fred. They were special to us, but there were others. At some point in our lives, Adam and I dismissed middle class, heterosexual morals. We figured we were gay and we had to establish our own rules. We also came to the conclusion that a good fuck did not erase deep love."

They were silent for a moment and Jim started to grin."

"OK. What's on your mind?" Adam asked.

"After Blake died, I was all right with celibacy for a short while, but I began to get itchy. I started a series of one night stands with guys I met on Silver Daddies. I'd be less than honest if I told you that I didn't have fun. I had a lot of fun, but until you came along, I wouldn't have considered a relationship with any of them.

"One night I went to a gay bar in West Hollywood. The clientele there are, shall we say, more mature men. I got to talking to a really handsome guy in his early sixties, probably a bit younger than Billy and Fred. I was flattered at the attention he paid me and his obvious flirting with me. It turned out that he was from Phoenix and he came to LA on business a couple of times a month. His average stay was two or three nights. He came home with me that first night and we had fantastic sex. He is still able to fuck me.

"To make a long story short, Russ is married and soon to be a grandfather for the first time. He would never leave his wife, so there could never be anything more between us than sex. Since I met you, he and I get together whenever he is in town. I don't want to have any secrets between us. I told him I couldn't see him again after you moved out here, and the poor guy began to cry. He still has sex with his wife, but his true nature is to have sex with a man. He begged me to ask you, if we could do a threesome. I told him I'd ask you, but I would do whatever you decided."

"I can't even imagine how frustrating this man's life must be," Adam said. He ran his palm down Jim's cheek. "Anyway, you had me when you said that he could still fuck. When is he coming again?"

Jim smiled. "He's coming Sunday evening and staying until Wednesday evening. I'll call him on his cell phone and tell him to come straight here when he gets his rental car at the airport. He gets all his calls on his cell phone, so his wife or his boss wouldn't know that he's not at his hotel if they should call. He says that his accounting department would be pleased if they didn't see any hotel expenses. Our perk is that he can offset that by taking us out on his expense account." That struck Jim funny and he laughed. He reached into his wallet and pulled out a picture of Russ. Adam had to agree that he was indeed a hunk. Looking at his picture, however, made Adam uneasy. He wasn't quite sure why.

Jim then picked up his land line and called Russ on his cell phone. He told him that Adam was agreeable and that he should come here directly from the airport. Then he looked at Adam who was smiling. He handed Adam the phone and said, "Russ wants to talk to you."

Adam was surprised but he took the phone and said, "Hi Russ."

"Hello," Russ said. Adam's body stiffened. There was something in Russ's voice that deeply disturbed him. "I just needed to thank you and to tell you that Jim is madly in love with you. You are all he speaks about when we are passionately engaged. If I was free, I'd be jealous, but as you know, I have no right to be. I hope you won't judge me because of my situation. I need sympathy and understanding, not to be told that I am a philanderer."

"I do understand, and I am sympathetic."

"Thank you, Adam. I can't wait to meet you Sunday evening, Ciao!" Adam hung up the phone.

"Thank you," Jim said, "for being you. If the situation with Russ turns out to be too much for the three of us to handle, I'll cut him off. I promise."

"Relax," Adam said. "I have a feeling it will be just fine." He took Jim in his arms and they kissed tenderly.

"I am so thrilled that you are here," Jim said. "Now I can look forward to each new day because we'll be together." Just then the phone rang and Jim answered.

"Hello," he said.... "Hi, how are you doing?... Sure, no problem. We'll be there at seven. That was Billy," he said. "We are picking him up at seven and he asked his 'friend' to join us, but don't let on that you know they are more than that. Let Billy tell you himself if he wants to."

"That's no problem," Adam said. "What is a problem is that if we pick them up at seven, we probably won't eat until eight or nine o'clock, maybe later. It will take some getting used to, eating dinner so much later than I am accustomed to. Which reminds me, it's three hours later in Florida, and I am starved. What can I have to tide me over?"

"I've got just the thing," Jim said. "How about coffee with a piece of apple pie. You can have some ice cream on it if you wish. After that we still have plenty of time to play before dinner."

"Sounds like a perfect plan to me," Adam said.

After their snack, they returned to the bedroom. They cuddled, fondled, sucked and rimmed. It was all their old bodies could do. Neither of them came again, but they didn't care. They were happy with what they did, and happier still just loving each other.

On the way to Billy's house, Jim said, "Billy's friend Juan is only forty-two years old. His father was Mexican and his mother was a total WASP. Her family disowned her when she married Juan Lopez, Sr. but he provided for her really well. He owned one of the biggest landscaping companies in Los Angeles. It belongs to Juan now. His mixed blood gives him a really exotic look. He's one handsome dude. When Fred is home, Juan shares a bed with both of them, and when Billy is in Sacramento, Fred's friend, Jonathan, shares a bed with Fred and Billy. I hope you aren't too shocked."

"Not at all," Adam said, and he proceeded to tell Jim all about Hans and Barry, and the love they all had for each other. "That's why I am not shocked about Russ, either. Love is love, and should never be denied. I get that you have feelings for Russ. If I deny that, you might resent me subconsciously, so I'd rather have the opportunity to learn to love Russ also."

"You are one hell of a guy," Jim said as he pulled into Billy's driveway. He honked his horn and in a few moments Billy came out with Juan. Adam jumped out of the car to embrace Billy. Introductions were made and Jim had been a hundred percent correct. Juan was absolutely beautiful. Lucky Billy and Fred. Adam wondered what Jonathan looked like.

Jim drove to Wolfgang Puck, a longtime favorite restaurant in LA. After they were seated Billy reminded them that dinner was on him and they better order what they liked and not to pay attention to the prices on the menu. "I am so thrilled and happy to have Adam here in LA with me, and living with one of my best friends. It calls for a celebration of epic proportions, and I mean it, so eat up, my friends."

"So what are we doing here?" Jim asked. "Shouldn't we have gone to McDonalds?" That cracked everyone up.

During dinner there was no denying the sexual tension between Juan and Billy. Adam couldn't help but wonder what Juan was getting out of this relationship. Maybe he was one of those guys who avoided commitment and this was as good as he wanted it to get. Billy was aware that Adam was studying them closely so when Juan excused himself for a few minutes, Billy said, "Adam, there's something you should know."

Adam interrupted him. "You don't have to say a word Billy. Any idiot could see what is going on. He seems like a great guy, and you owe me no explanations."

Billy asked Jim, "Didn't I tell you he was the most understanding, kindest guy in the world? I lost my real father, but Adam will always be a father to me also."

Adam took Billy's hand and squeezed it.

After Jim dropped Juan and Billy off at Billy's house and started for home, he said to Adam, "You are an amazing soul Adam. I thank God that I met you." Adam leaned over and kissed Jim on the cheek.

That night in bed they cuddled as close to each other as possible. They didn't have sex again, but each fell asleep assured that their futures together would be wonderful, whether it would be for another day or another twenty years.

CHAPTER ELEVEN

During the next few days, Adam finished his unpacking, and he and Jim rearranged the closets and the dresser drawers. They packed five of Adam's twelve clothing boxes with clothes that they both decided should be discarded, and called an AID's charity to take them away. Slowly Adam got over his jet lag, and began to adapt to his new environment. He was even getting used to eating dinner hours later than he did in Florida.

In Florida, he needed to drive somewhere for every amenity, and in the last year he had depended on Jamie for wheels. Here in Jim's neighborhood, he could walk to plenty of adequate shopping strip malls. There seemed to be one on every street corner. Adam loved to walk, and the new exercise was great for him. He lost five pounds and felt wonderful. Jim began to walk with him and he prayed that Jim would not lose his love handles.

Adam's first Sunday in LA arrived much too quickly, and Adam began to get nervous about Russ. His agitation did not escape Jim, who took Adam in his arms and said, "It's not too late. If you say no, I'll send him to a hotel."

"Nonsense, I wouldn't let you be so cruel.   However, I wouldn't mind if you described his body to me."

Jim did not realize that Adam was joking and he began to speak. Adam broke out laughing and shut him up. "I love how naïve you can be sometimes. I was just kidding."

They expected Russ about 9 PM, and about 9:15 a car pulled up in the driveway. A man got out of the front seat and opened the back door. He removed a suitcase and headed for the house. Adam was looking at him through the living room window as Jim went to greet him at the front door. All at once Adam got the same disturbed feeling he had gotten when he first saw Russ's picture. In a moment he would know why.

Russ came in and Jim immediately closed the front door. Russ dropped his suitcase and he and Jim embraced and kissed on the lips. Jim grabbed Russ's hand and said, "Come. I want you to meet Adam."

Adam did a double take. Russ had the same skin coloring and color eyes as Evan. His frame was also the same as Evan's, as was his height. His resemblance to Evan was uncanny in every way. Adam thought that if he was uncut and the same cock size as Evan, he would pass right out. Russ could easily have passed as Evan's son. He composed himself and stuck his hand out, but Russ would have none of that. He grabbed Adam in a bear hug and kissed him on the lips. For a split second, Adam dreamt that he was being kissed by Evan and he responded to Russ's kiss in a big way.

"Adam," Russ said, "Thank you for allowing me to be here. My time with Jim is so precious to me and now I hope it will be that way with the two of you."

My God! Adam thought. *He even sounds like Evan.* He could not control himself.

"Russ," he asked. "Are there any Morrisseys in your family?"

"Not that I know of," Russ answered. "Why do you ask?"

Adam reached into his wallet and took out a picture taken on his tour of Europe with Evan. At the time Evan would have been a couple of years older than Russ. He and Evan were on the right and Hans and Barry were on their left. They all had their arms around each other. "Does anyone in this picture look familiar to you?" Adam asked.

Russ studied the picture carefully. Then he pointed to Evan. "This guy here could pass as my brother," he said.

"Thank you," Adam said. "I thought I was going crazy. The man you pointed to was my partner. He passed away a few months ago."

"Sorry," Russ mumbled. He was feeling uncomfortable for the first time.

"It's Ok. I just got a little jolt, is all. I'll be fine. Excuse me for a minute, please. I'll be right back." Adam went to the bedroom and faced the mirror. He looked at his reflection and talked to it.

"No it's impossible," he thought. "What could the odds be?"

———————

It was a couple of years after Adam and Evan moved to Miami. They were managing to get by, but a little extra spending money would certainly be welcome. One evening Evan came home with a shit eaten grin on his face. He tossed five crisp ten dollar bills on the kitchen table. With a flourish of his arms, he said, "Tada!!"

"Did you rob a bank?" Adam asked sarcastically.

"No, I jerked off in a bottle and they paid me top dollar at the sperm bank."

"No shit. Why top dollar?" Adam asked.

"Because I have a rare blood type. It's B Positive." One of the guys at work put me on to it. They pay anywhere from $25 to $50 depending on your blood type. You can only donate once a month and no more than six times. They figure that with only six donations, even if all six are successful, the odds of a brother and sister getting it on in later years are almost impossible. Wanna come with me next time?"

"Sure, but I'm O Positive. That's the most common. I guess all I could get would be $25," Adam lamented.

"You've done it hundreds of time for free so don't scoff at $25. We could walk away with $75 to $100 between us. Not bad for a hand job."

Over the next six months they each donated to the sperm bank once a month. Adam was correct. He only got $25. Still it was $25 they didn't have before.

———————

Adam went downstairs. Russ and Jim were standing in the middle of the kitchen kissing. Their hands were on the other's crotch. Adam didn't even notice. "Are you OK?" Jim asked. He and Russ looked very concerned.

"Please let's sit down," Adam said. They sat at the kitchen table. Adam took hold of Russ's hand. "Russ, I need to ask you some questions. They are going to sound strange to you, but please answer as best you can. I'll explain why later."

"Sure," Russ said. "I owe you Adam."

Adam began. "Do you know what your blood type is?"

"Of course. It's B Positive." Adam shivered.

"Were your parents or maybe just your mother ever in the Miami area?"

"That's a really uncanny question. How did you know? My grandparents lived in Miami. My folks moved to LA when my dad got transferred there right after they were married. I never got the whole story, but my mom once told me that she and my dad had a lot of stress in the early days of their marriage. They were trying hard for two years to get pregnant and it wasn't happening so my mother felt that they needed a vacation from each other. She went back to Miami to be with her folks. She said she would stay two weeks but she stayed two months.

"When she came home she finally got pregnant, but things didn't change between them. My dad quit his job and disappeared one day, leaving his pregnant wife to make it on her own. She told me that she wanted to go back to Florida, but her pregnancy was touch and go, so she couldn't travel. There was a young woman in our building who befriended my mother. She helped her through the pregnancy and afterwards, my mom and I moved in with her. I don't tell this to a lot of people but my mom and Eleanor became lovers. I was raised by two fantastic moms."

Adam was speechless. He didn't know what to say. Russ's mother must have gone to the sperm bank when she was in Miami. How could he tell this man that his father was not his father? In reality his father never was a father. Russ didn't even know him. If Evan was his father, Adam could tell him what a kind and loving man his real father was. It might be a blessing to Russ.

"Are you going to tell me now why you asked these questions?" Russ asked.

Falteringly, not knowing exactly the right words to use, Adam told Russ and Jim his suspicions and about the sperm bank. Now they were speechless.

"I have a couple of Evan's baseball caps," Adam said. "If we can find a hair or two inside, would you be willing to submit to a DNA test?"

"I don't know," Russ answered. "What kind of man was he?"

"He was a war hero, and the kindest, most altruistic man I ever knew. You saw his picture. He was also the handsomest man I ever knew. Men and women were always coming on to him. I'm sure he cheated on me a lot, but I didn't care. He was mine. He loved me and I knew he would always come home to our bed."

"In that case, please let's do it. I'd be so proud if he was my father. If he was, I'd want my kids to know. I'll have to think up a yarn to tell them how it all came about."

"My God," Adam said. "Making love to you tonight will be like making love to Evan again."

"Should I be jealous?" Jim asked.

"Not on your life," Adam said and kissed Jim.

"My goal is to make you both happy," Russ added, and he did. That night Jim and Adam sucked his cock until he was good and hard. He put on a rubber, greased both their asses and his cock, and fucked them both. He would stop when he felt himself cumming and then he would switch assholes. After a while of course he had to cum and it was Adam who got the honors. Adam was sorry that Russ's spunk was captured by a condom. He would have enjoyed the old feeling of jism filling him up. In the next two days they all went down on each other in every combination.

Before he left on Wednesday, Russ gave Adam a lock of his hair. Adam put it in a small box and labeled it. With tweezers, he extracted two hairs from Evan's baseball cap. He put it in another small box and labeled it. He searched the yellow pages and found a lab that did DNA testing. It wasn't cheap, but he brought the samples in. They said that it would take about six weeks. The results had not yet arrived before Russ's next visit. This time all the stress of a threesome was gone, and the sex between them was fantastic.

One week after Russ's latest visit, the lab results were delivered. With a certainty of 99.8% it was determined that Sample B was the biological father of Sample A. For two days Adam read the results over and over, crying and laughing alternately. Evan had a son. He left a legacy, and Adam had made love to that son many times. He was elated. He longed to tell Evan, Barry and Hans, but they were all gone. Did they know the truth in whatever realm they dwelt? He prayed that they did.

When his composure returned, he phoned Billy and told him about Russ. Billy was flabbergasted. "Hey," he said, "if he looks like Evan, I want in on the action." Was he kidding? Adam wasn't sure. He begged Jim to call Russ, but Jim preferred to wait until Russ's next visit.

"We'll go out for a fine dinner and spring the news on him," Jim said.

"We'll have to ask Billy too, and Fred if he's in town. Billy is dying to meet Evan's son."

Even though they didn't call Russ, he sensed that the DNA results would be in by now. He told his wife that he was having difficulty with plane reservations and couldn't get his usual flight to LA, so he had to leave on the same flight but on Saturday evening instead of Sunday. She didn't mind at all.

When he arrived, the first thing he did was ask about the DNA. "We received the results, but we haven't opened the envelope," Jim lied. "We are all going out to dinner tonight, including Adam's spiritual son, Billy. We'll open the envelope then and we'll celebrate no matter what the results are."

"OK, but what is a spiritual son?" I don't know what that means," Russ said.

"I don't know either," Adam lamented, "but I'll tell you all about Billy, Evan and me, and I think you'll understand." Adam held back nothing concerning Billy, including how he seduced Evan when he was sixteen.

"Even though I'm a few years younger than Billy, if the results prove that Evan was my father, I guess that makes me your son too, and Billy and I are brothers," Russ philosophized.

"I guess so, and I will be proud to include you in our small family," Adam said with a crack in his voice.

"I wonder if there is a way to find out if you and Evan fathered any more children." Jim wondered.

"It's best not to know, and I'm not going to expend an effort to find out." Adam stated firmly.

Much to Juan's disappointment, Billy told him he couldn't have dinner with him this evening, because people would be present whom he didn't want to know about his extra marital affair. "It's none of their business," Juan moped, "but I'll respect your wishes."

Billy gasped when he met Russ. "If Evan isn't your father," he said, "then someone in heaven accidently repeated Evan's gene pool. I'm not only looking at Evan's double, I'm hot for him too. Heaven help me."

"Well, you made out with my maybe father. What's to stop you from making out with his son?" Billy blushed and kissed Russ on the cheek. "That would be really great," he said.

Halfway through the entrée, Russ lost his patience. "For God's sake, Adam, open the freaking letter before I bust."

"Are you sure?" Adam asked. "If the news is bad, I don't want you to lose your appetite. This meal is too expensive and its on Jim and me."

"If I lose my appetite, I'll pay for my own dinner. Just please open it up." Adam took the resealed letter from his breast pocket and opened it up. Nothing on his face betrayed the results, whether good or bad. He handed the letter to Russ.

"I guess you better read it yourself."

Russ started to read and after the first few seconds, his shoulders began to heave, then his whole body started to shake. The other three men knew the results and said nothing. They wanted Russ to talk first.

Finally, he folded the letter and put it in his pocket. Then quietly he said, "When my mother and Eleanor died, I had no family except my wife and two sons. My sons have wives of their own now, and live hundreds of miles from me and from each other. All I have is my wife, and as much as I'd like to come out, I need to protect her. I have a whole new family now. It's not a blood family, but it's my family none the less."

Everyone stood up, and one by one they embraced Russ. Soon the somber mood disappeared and the celebration began. They were joyous and ordered a bottle of champagne, which was consumed rather quickly.

Billy must have been feeling a little high when he said, "Adam and Jim, you will have Russ until Wednesday. How about letting him come home with me tonight so I can get better acquainted with my brother?"

"That's entirely up to Russ," Jim said.

"I think I'd like that very much," Russ responded.

CHAPTER TWELVE

Adam and Jamie spoke on the phone every Sunday evening at 5 PM, Pacific Time, and 8 PM, Eastern Time. They didn't have to restrict their activities to make time for these calls, thanks to cell phones. One time Jamie and Tim had tickets to a Sunday evening concert given by The Gay Men's Chorus of Ft. Lauderdale. Jamie actually left the theater just before eight to take Adam's call.

Adam had once told Jamie all about his relationship with Hans and Barry. In turn Jamie had relayed the story to Tim. They were returning from a New Year party and Jamie said, "I love Adam. What would you say if I told you that I would welcome us having a relationship with Jim and him, like he and Evan had with Hans and Barry?"

Tim planted a kiss on Jamie's lips. "I would say that they are coming here next month and we should go for it if it's OK with them."

"Somehow I think it will be," Jamie said.

Adam and Jim booked themselves on a flight to Ft. Lauderdale on Feb.10ᵗʰ. Their return trip was open ended. They didn't want any time restrictions put on their sojourn in Sunny Florida. Jamie and Tim were waiting anxiously in the terminal for their arrival. They were both very nervous about asking Adam and Jim to share their bed as well as their board. Jamie was particularly nervous. The only man he had ever slept with in his life was Tim. They decided to give it a day or two before broaching the subject.

Due to the time difference, Adam and Jim's flight did not arrive until early evening. They were starved when Jamie and Tim picked them up, and they went straight to what was Adam's favorite restaurant until his recent move. The restaurant was located in Wilton Manors, the gayest section of Ft. Lauderdale. Jim was amazed. None of this had been here when he moved away so many years ago. They ate and left quickly without socializing since Adam and Jim were worn out by the long trip.

Jamie and Tim lived in a two bedroom home. The two bedrooms and their baths were at opposite ends of the house so that guests had complete privacy. After Adam and Jim were settled in their bedroom, the four men sat around the living room talking. Jamie decided to test the waters.

"Back in good old Sunnydale," he said, "Adam and I saw each other naked on a few occasions, so I hope it will be all right with you two gents that Tim and I parade around naked."

"Not at all," Jim said. "We do the same."

"You know," Jamie said, "even when I thought I was straight, I hungered after that big cock of yours, Adam."

"Too bad you didn't say something then," Adam said. "Evan and I were always up for a threesome. We would have enjoyed breaking you in."

"I had that pleasure," Tim interjected.

"Lucky you," Jim added.

The seeds were sown. They began to grow the next morning.

At nine o'clock, Adam and Jim were still asleep. They had not yet adjusted to the time difference. Jamie and Tim came into their room in their birthday suits and rudely started awakening them. They were naked too of course. Unfortunately at their ages, neither Adam nor Jim had morning woodies, but both were somewhat engorged.

"Come on you guys," Tim said. "Half the day is gone." He jumped into their bed and started wrestling with them. Jamie followed suit. They were giggling like kids and grabbing for each other's cocks. Nobody tried to stop anybody else, but finally Jim said, "If I don't pee soon, I'm going to wet the bed."

"Me too," Adam echoed.

"OK," Jamie said, "We'll continue this later."

"Sounds like fun," Jim said.

The seedlings were full grown and blossoming.

―――――――――

They landed at Shannon Airport and were met by their tour guide. Besides Adam, Evan, Hans and Barry there were twenty other people in their group. The tour guide told them in a thick Irish brogue that he would be with them in Ireland and England, but another guide would pick them up when they crossed the channel. He instructed them to leave their luggage next to the bus and the driver would load it. He said that they would be leaving in exactly one hour and told them that they could browse the duty free shops in the meantime, but please not to be late for their departure.

"So that's why they fly us to Shannon and bus us to Dublin." Hans said. "Shannon's duty free shops are well known to all travelers."

They browsed as instructed, but bought nothing. Anything they bought would have to be schlepped for the duration of the trip. They agreed to buy cautiously and late in the trip.

On the way to Dublin, the guide pointed out places of interest along the way. They arrived in Dublin in time for dinner. After they were assigned their rooms they all assembled for dinner in the hotel dining room. After dinner they were free until the next morning when they would be given a half day tour of the city. The rest of that day and the next were free until they would leave for London. Evan took his gay guide to Dublin out of his pocket. They chose a likely looking gay pub, engaged a taxi driver and set off. It turned out that the pub was walking distance from the hotel, a fact that the taxi driver neglected to tell them.

The pub was very noisy and the music was loud. The patrons were all very young and nobody paid any attention to them. They each ordered a pint of beer, and afterward they decided to walk back to their hotel. Now that they were all four making love to each other, they knew that the action back at the hotel would be great.

Each of their rooms had twin beds so they tossed a coin. Adam and Hans started in one bed and Evan and Barry in the other in the same room. They changed partners often and when they were exhausted, each couple slept in a twin bed rather than return to the other room. Since Evan did not ejaculate, Hans and Barry made jokes about how neat and clean he was. They had melded into one body and one soul. At that point in time if someone had told Adam that he would outlive them all and be left alone, he might well have killed himself.

———————

After breakfast Tim and Jamie took Adam to see his old street in Hollywood. Nothing had changed much except the trees were bigger and more beautiful than ever. They drove to Miami and South Beach and Jim was amazed. He had left a sleepy little city and returned to a megalopolis. They ate a big lunch in South Beach at an outdoor café and enjoyed the eye candy. The lunch was more than any of them usually ate and they decided that dinner would be a cup of coffee and maybe some toast at home. They were all anxious to get home anyway. There was no doubt that they would all have something more for dinner than a cup of coffee and toast.

Arriving at home they rushed into Jamie and Tim's bedroom, undressed rapidly and plopped down on the big king size bed. None of them had a good hard erection, but all of them were engorged.

"I want to make love to you Adam," Jamie said. "I guess I have loved you secretly, maybe subconsciously, for a very long time." He rolled over on top of Adam and their lips met. They kissed and fondled for a long time. Then Jamie moved down and took Adam's cock into his mouth. By that time, Jim was making Tim equally as happy. Jamie and Jim continued sucking until Adam and Tim came in their mouths. There was a bit of a rest and they changed positions. When everyone was happy and satisfied, they all showered and dressed and went to Wilton Manors for dinner. Apparently their appetites had been revived.

Adam and Jim remained in Florida for about three weeks. The four friends had more fun together than they had dared hope for. Jamie and Tim planned to visit them in LA in the middle of August and stay until after Labor Day for as long as they all felt like it. They decided to say their farewells at home because the tears were flowing like Niagara Falls, so Adam and Jim took a cab to the airport.

They had a 2 PM flight, and arrived at the airport at about 11:45 AM. With all the delays getting through security, they still had time for lunch before boarding the plane. During lunch Jim asked, "The love the four of us enjoyed was amazing wasn't it?"

"It was more than physical," Adam answered, "It was spiritual, at least to me."

"I agree," Jim concurred. "The way you felt about Jamie and later Tim, is the same way I feel about Billy and Fred. Do you think they would want to become physical with us?"

"I'm sure Billy would. He has hinted, but this would be complicated because Juan and Jonathan are also in the picture," Adam mused.

"Yes, it is rather convoluted," Jim agreed, "But it sure would be interesting to see what kind of a scenario we could concoct about this one. There would be six of us, so wow."

It was their last day in Rome. The four lovers went to a restaurant that the gay guide book had recommended. They were more than pleasantly pleased. The patrons were all mature men. A string quartet was playing lovely music in the background. It was a quiet and perfect place to enjoy a wonderfully satisfying dinner.

The food lived up to expectations too. Since they could not make up their minds what to order from such a savory assortment, the beautiful young waiter recommended that they order the sampler plate for dinner, and have a taste of a variety of entrees. They did just that. During dinner they simply oohed and aahed as each course was served. This meal was the highlight of their stay in Europe.

As they were sipping cappuccinos, a handsome couple came over to their table. They were about the same age as the four tourists.

"Excuse me, gentlemen," one of them said. "We couldn't help overhearing some of your conversation. You are Americans, si?"

"Yes, we are, and we are in love with your country," Hans said. Hans had become their unofficial spokesman in Europe for no other reason than he was born there.

"We would be honored if you gentlemen would allow us to provide you with after dinner drinks at the bar when you are finished with your meal," the other of them said.

"We would be the honored ones," Hans said very diplomatically.

"I am Mario," the first gentleman said, "and my partner is Guido." Mario extended his hand which Hans shook, and then he made introductions around the table. When they finished eating and went to the bar, they saw that Mario and Guido had set them up at a table for six in a quiet corner.

Mario waved to the waiter, who came over and took their order. The six chatted for a while and each couple gave a short biography of their lives together. Their conversation was comfortable and enjoyable.

"Gentlemen," Mario said. "In about an hour a small group of our friends are gathering at our apartment for a little party. We would be so pleased if you would join us also."

"You seem very nice," Hans said, "and we have no reason to suspect that your motives are anything but the best. However, I would feel more comfortable if I knew exactly the kind of party you have in mind."

Guido laughed. "I think you have already figured it out, Hans."

Now it was Hans's turn to laugh. He looked at his companions and smiled. "I think that Mario and Guido are inviting us to sex party. It sounds like fun to me."

The others weren't so sure, but Evan who was always up to more and more sex and especially kinky sex, said, "Sure why not?" Adam and Barry just naturally fell into line."

"How many others will be there?" Evan asked.

"Four more. There will be ten of us altogether," Mario said. "Please don't worry. We are not into bondage or leather or anything like that. We just like to enjoy sex with a variety of men with a variety of sizes. We will provide adequate protection."

The ten men ranged in age from 35 to 65. At first they sat around sipping the wine their hosts had provided. All but two of the men spoke English, and the others translated for them. After two or three glasses had been consumed, one of the younger men came over to Evan and took his hand. He led him into one of three bedrooms and began to kiss him. Evan eagerly responded and they began to undress. When they were naked, Alfredo said that they should try to stay on one side of the bed because shortly another couple would join them and use the other side. In less than ten minutes there were five couples performing various sexual acts all over the apartment. Nobody was with their own partner. After five minutes Alfredo's partner, Gino, interrupted Evan and Alfredo, and Gino took over for Alfredo. And so it went. The ten men switched partners often. Evan came twice. Adam came only once, but they kept switching partners and nobody could remember who they were with when they achieved orgasm. Evan even had Adam for a short while.

As promised there were no kinky things going on, just pure love making. Our American foursome enjoyed themselves thoroughly. They thanked their hosts profusely and in the taxi ride back to their hotel, they could not stop discussing their good fortune. They even got a promise from Guido and Mario that they would visit them in Florida one day. They never did.

———————————

"The way you felt about Jamie and later Tim, is the same way I feel about Billy and Fred. Do you think they would want to become physical with us?" Jim asked.

"I'm sure Billy would. He has hinted, but this would be complicated because Juan and Jonathan are also in the picture," Adam mused.

"Yes, it is rather convoluted," Jim agreed, "But it sure would be interesting to see what kind of a scenario we could concoct about this one. There would be six of us, so wow."

"I am sure I can create a scenario," Adam said to Jim, as he remembered the sex party in Rome. "Remind me to tell you about one fantastic night in Rome."

CHAPTER THIRTEEN

In the end Adam didn't have to concoct anything. He simply called Billy shortly after they returned to Florida and told him what had transpired in Florida. After thinking about it for awhile he also related the story of the sex party in Rome. Then he asked if he and Fred would like to have such a party. Billy didn't hesitate.

"I had Evan once and now I have the opportunity to make love to you, hopefully more than once. I don't expect Fred home for at least another three weeks. I can't wait that long. Can I come over very soon, and can I bring Juan?"

"At the risk of sounding like the slut I am," Adam answered, "in this instance the more the merrier. How does this Saturday or Sunday evening sound to you?"

"I'll check with Juan and get back to you. If he's not interested, I'll be over both nights by myself."

The foursome eventually agreed on Sunday evening to begin their new relationship. On Wednesday, Russ called to tell them that he would be arriving on Sunday evening until Wednesday. Adam and Jim were delighted.

"Everyone but us is young enough, and gets hard enough to fuck. We'll have a ball," Jim predicted.

Adam was always a little reticent about everything and simply answered, "I hope so. But don't you think that five will be a little awkward?"

"You always sound like a naïve little puppy," Jim said. "Haven't you ever enjoyed a threesome?"

"Of course," Adam answered. "I wasn't thinking."

———————

Adam thought back to a very exciting time when he and Evan enjoyed a very hot threesome. They had been living in Florida for about three years and had not returned to New Brunswick in all that time to visit Adam's family. Mike and Bob were now in college at Rutgers. Adam and Evan were feeling guilty and arranged their vacations at the same time so they could get back east. It was to be their last visit there until they passed through New York on their way to Europe in their sixties.

The flight made a stop in Atlanta and another in Philadelphia before landing at Newark Airport. There were no jets yet and the propeller driven motor needed these stops for change of passengers, and refueling.

They spent two fun filled days visiting with their parents and kid brothers, but on the third day they decided to visit their old campus and Greenwich Village.

They arrived at Penn Station at about 5:30 in the evening, and immediately took a subway to the NYU campus. They walked around campus for a bit, and were happy to note that nothing seemed to have changed. Once satisfied about that, they started to stroll toward The Village. They decided to have dinner at a small bistro, The Wine Cellar, where they used to eat at occasionally, when they could afford it. They would then have a few drinks at The Male Room and maybe dance a little. They intended to make the 11:30 back to New Brunswick. That was the last train out in the evening.

When they arrived at The Wine Cellar it was still a bit early for dinner and they had no trouble getting a table. After they were seated a young man, no more than nineteen years old, approached their table.

"Hi," he said, "I'm Anthony and I'll be your server this evening." He wore a name tag which said, 'Tony.' He handed them menus and asked if he could get them a drink before dinner. Evan ordered a scotch and soda and Adam, who rarely drank, ordered his old standby, a whiskey sour.

When Tony brought their drinks, he said, "Just call me when you are ready to order." He seemed to be about to leave, but he didn't. Instead he asked, "Are you students at the university? You look a little old to be students."

"No," Adam said. "We're alumni. We graduated three years ago. Are you a student?"

Tony nodded. "Yes, I'm in my sophomore year. I'm majoring in Journalism."

Adam and Evan smiled at him, but he seemed disinclined to leave. It seemed he wanted to say more, but he was a little hesitant. Finally he screwed up his courage and asked. "Are you two guys a couple?"

Adam took hold of Evan's hand, nodded, smiled and said, "You bet we are." He leaned over and kissed Evan lightly on the lips. Tony smiled back and left the table.

Later Tony took their order and every time he was at their table, he tried to make some small talk. Evan remarked to Adam that they were getting more attention than was necessary. "I think he's hot for you." Adam remarked.

"Bull," Evan responded, "he's hot for you."

"Maybe he's hot for both of us."

When Tony cleared the table and handed them their bill, he casually remarked that his shift ended at nine. Evan couldn't care less, but Adam was flattered at the attention the young man was bestowing on them so he said, "We're going to The Male Room from here. I don't know how long we'll be there, but if you come on by after work, look for us."

"You bet," Tony said.

The only thing that had changed at The Male Room was the music. The sensual ballads of the forties were not the only music played there now. Early signs of rock and roll were creeping in, and couples were gyrating to such songs as Rock Around The Clock and Rockin' Robin. Adam and Evan danced close to each other to the ballads, but sat out watching the young boys gyrate to the rock and roll rhythms. Finally they tried their hand, or rather their feet, at one of the fast numbers. They were rather inept, but they had fun and a few good laughs.

They were having a ball and didn't realize the passage of time. They came off the dance floor and there was Tony smiling at them.

"Hi kid," Adam said. "We have a small table over there. Wanna join us?"

Tony nodded and followed them to the table. "I'm nineteen he said so would one of you buy me a drink? I'd be much obliged," he said as he pulled out his wallet.

"It's OK," Evan said. "It's on us. What's your poison?"

"Seven and Seven," Tony said, trying to sound very suave and debonair.

Evan was nursing another scotch and soda, Adam was sipping another whiskey sour and Tony was merely putting his lips to his drink, when Tony cleared his throat and asked, "Can I confess something to you guys confidentially?"

"Can't promise a thing," Evan said glibly. "We aren't catholic priests, but shoot away."

Tony leaned forward so they could hear him better, and hardly above a whisper he said, "I think I might be homosexual."

Evan's answer to this statement, which Adam had heard often enough, and which he would hear many times in the future, was always the same, "You think? You don't know?"

"Well, I'm pretty sure."

"Have you had sex yet or are you still a virgin?" Adam was always the curious one.

"I've had sex once, with a girl, on my prom night. I had to do it. It was expected," Tony said.

"How did you manage?" Adam was getting more curious.

Without hesitating, Tony said, "I fantasized I was with a hot guy like either of you two."

Adam and Evan began to laugh. "Flattery will get you everywhere," Evan said leading the boy on. Adam gave Evan a look that said, "Are you crazy?"

Encouraged, Tony said, "Please fellows, I'm afraid to approach anyone here and nobody ever approaches me. I tell you, I am getting desperate and damn tired of whacking off to fantasies that aren't coming true. Would you guys give a thought to breaking me in?"

Adam was hesitant. "What do you mean nobody ever approached you? You're damn good looking," he said.

"Adam," Evan said, "do you remember that night at the baths?"

Adam remembered all right. His cock began to stiffen.

"We don't have to go to any baths," Tony said. "My roommate dropped out of school a couple of weeks ago and I am a single right now."

Adam smiled. "You mean we can fool around in the dorms again. I'm getting more interested."

Evan looked at his watch. It was 10:15. "We'll never make the 11:30," he said.

"I saw a pay phone in the lobby," Adam said. "I'll call home and tell them we met some old school chums and are spending the night in the big apple." He left but returned very shortly.

They finished their drinks and they each had one more. They all needed some liquid encouragement. They walked back to the old familiar dorms with Tony. Entering the building, Tony was a nervous wreck. He looked up and down the halls and when the coast was clear, he rushed them into his room. Adam was filled with déjà vu. Tony's room turned out to be right next door to the one Adam had occupied in his lower freshman year.

Adam and Evan sat down on one of the beds and neither made any indication that they would start the evening's activities. Tony just stood there, frozen in time and space. Finally Evan stood up, put his arms around the boy and started to kiss him. Tony began to relax, and he fairly melted when Adam began to play with the bulge in his pants.

"I think we should get undressed," Adam said in his practical business voice.

Evan smiled at Tony and they all started to undress. When they were all naked, Tony stared at Adam's cock in near disbelief. He and Evan were more near average, but Adam had a whopper. Evan saw Tony staring at his partner's well-endowed asset and said, "You should feel how great that monster feels up your ass." Tony turned white.

"Lie down on the bed," Adam instructed. Tony lay down on his back as instructed, and the two old hands began to give him a trip around the world. Tony began to show musical talent as he sighed and moaned in joy and pleasure.

Evan was the first to take Tony's cock into his mouth. After a few strokes, he began to turn around into a sixty-nine position. Tony knew what was expected and tried to use his lips and tongue just as Evan was doing. Evan was lying on top of Tony and Adam began to suck his balls and rim his asshole. It was Evan's turn to moan in pleasure.

Evan and Tony came almost simultaneously. They continued sucking until each began to soften. Then Adam lay on his back and Tony and Evan began their trips around Adam's world. They sucked Adam alternately, but Evan allowed Adam to cum in Tony's mouth. The three lay in a bundled crunch catching their breaths. Finally Evan asked Tony if he had any lube. Nobody used condoms in those days.

"Sure," Tony said. "I use a little when I whack off."

"Adam is going to fuck you first with his big salami and then you can fuck either or both of us. How does that sound?"

"Like dreams coming true," Tony sighed.

Evan and Adam spent a good deal of time greasing and stretching Tony until they felt it was time for Adam's big entry. They warned him that it would hurt a lot at first, but advised him to stick with it because the end would justify the means.

Adam entered doggie style, and Tony stuffed his fist in his mouth. The pain was excruciating, but he did not stop Adam. When Adam was all the way in, he stayed perfectly still and whispered softly in Tony's ear, "Relax sweetie. The pain will leave, I promise, and you will experience sheer joy. Just relax as much as you can."

Adam could feel the young man relaxing a little at a time and he knew exactly when Tony passed the threshold of pain into pleasure. He began to stroke slowly and gently, and Tony began to laugh.

"What's so funny?" Adam asked.

"I feel like I have to shit."

"You better not," Adam said and all three of them started to laugh.

Tony's asshole was really tight and Evan instructed him to contract his muscles. Adam's lasting power was short. He spurted into Tony and then lay exhausted on top of him while trying to catch his breath.

Tony took a little longer to reach another climax. Adam and Evan greased their asses very generously and then Evan greased Tony's cock. He rubbed on the lube and Tony got as hard as a rock. He entered Evan first without any resistance. After a few strokes, he came out of Evan and gave his pleasure to Adam. He went back and forth this way, delaying his orgasm as long as he could. When he could hold back no longer he spurted into Adam. "Turnabout is fair play," he said.

Evan and Adam stayed the night. They slept in Tony's roommate's bed and Tony slept in his own bed. In the wee hours of the morning they awoke and formed a daisy chain, bringing each other to yet another climax. After that they all showered in the shower room where Evan had first admired Adam's ample endowments.

Before parting, they invited Tony to visit them in Florida anytime he could. Tony thanked them profusely for the best night of his life. On the train back to New Jersey, Adam and Evan congratulated themselves on breaking in yet another virgin.

————————

Billy called on Friday to confirm that he and Juan were coming over on Sunday evening. The four of them made up to have dinner together at a neighborhood restaurant, before spending the night at Jim's house. Jim was excited as hell. Adam was as nervous as hell. Billy was like a son to him and he felt that this was all a little incestual. He kept reminding himself that they were not blood related.

Billy and Juan drove to Jim's house, and from there they walked to the restaurant. To tell the truth they were all a bit nervous. As soon as they had ordered, Jim broke the ice.

"Listen guys," he said to Billy and Juan. "Adam and I don't get hard enough anymore to penetrate and we are counting on you two guys to give us that pleasure."

Billy turned a beet red, but Juan said, "It will be our pleasure." After that everyone seemed to relax a little and they chattered over dinner, told little anecdotes, and actually informed each other how excited they all were about what was about to transpire.

"We shouldn't start before Russ gets here in about an hour or so," Adam said.

Russ parked his rental car in the driveway and rushed into the house. He kissed everyone and said how thrilled he was to be here with his new family.

Adam made them all coffee and served the coffee with assorted pastries. Russ began to speak.

"I racked my brains trying to create a plausible story to tell my family about finding my birth father, and telling them what a great guy he was. Finally, I told my wife that I met a guy named Adam Langston at a luncheon with a business associate. I said he couldn't get over the resemblance I had to a late friend of his. Upon talking about it, I told him that my mother had gone to Miami for a couple of months about the time I was conceived. He and his friend lived there at the time. I told her that he said that he and his friend Evan had donated sperm about that time. I told her that you asked for a lock of my hair and that you ran a DNA test which proved that Evan Morrissey was indeed the donor. I told my wife that Evan was a war hero and a pillar in his community. All the while I believed the scoundrel who deserted my mother was my biological father, but now I could be proud of whom my father really was. My wife is thrilled for me. She called my sons and gave them the good news. They are equally pleased as punch. Adam, I am going to take this one step further. I am going to tell her, that you and I have become great friends and that you are like the father I never had. Is that OK with you? That way, I can call you freely from Phoenix without her being suspicious."

Adam embraced Russ. Every time he did that, it was as if Evan was back in his arms. "Make love to me, please," he whispered to Russ, "and I'll pretend I'm making love to your father again." Russ held Adam even tighter, and began to cry.

Billy interrupted. "Let's not be maudlin," he said. "Let's play instead." He took Jim's hand and started toward the bedroom. Juan, Adam and Russ followed suit. It was a night to remember for Jim and Adam. Billy, Juan and Russ each had their cocks in both of them, but by agreement, it was Russ who finally spilled inside of Adam and Billy came inside of Jim. To make up for being unable to fuck, Adam and Jim sucked all three of them to orgasm. As for anal sex, Billy, Juan and Russ took care of each other.

Adam finally fell peacefully asleep, having been fucked after a very long hiatus. More importantly he could now call Russ freely whenever he wanted to, and it would be like chatting with Evan.

Oh Evan, Adam thought, *I wish you could know what a fine son you have, and next month you will be a great grandfather.*

CHAPTER FOURTEEN

On their next visit to Ft. Lauderdale, Adam and Jim planned on staying two weeks, but ended up staying for a month. A few days before they were due to fly home, a severe earthquake struck the Los Angeles area. Their flight was cancelled, and Tim and Jamie were delighted.

Two days after the earthquake they were able to get a call through to Billy. He assured them that their home was in tact, but traffic was a mess. Most traffic lights were out and many streets were impassible, and would stay that way until they could be repaved. Billy advised them to stay in Florida for the immediate future. In spite of the bad conditions at home, they booked one of the first flights to LA after the airport was reopened.

On the evening before their departure, the four of them had a marvelous dinner at a four star restaurant, and then had a fantastic night of loving, mutual sex at home.

"I'm sure going to miss you guys," Tim said. "August seems a million years away."

"I know," Adam agreed. "But this is where fate has placed us and I guess this is where we were meant to be. Two visits a year are better than none."

"Amen," Jamie said.

The flight home was full. Most of the passengers were disgruntled. They should have been home days and weeks ago, and were now headed home, or on business, at the first opportunity which was presented to them. Adam and Jim had an aisle and middle seat in coach. A rather portly woman occupied the window seat. Some of her spilled over into Jim's seat, forcing him to raise the arm between his seat and Adam's, and cozying up to his partner. They secured a blanket and during the flight they covered themselves, so that they were able to fondle each other in relative obscurity. The portly woman slept most of the way and noticed nothing. Adam began to doze off.

———————

The Aer Lingus jet taking them to Shannon had two seats on the port and starboard sides, and six seats in the middle. Evan and Adam sat alone in 8A and 8B. Hans and Barry were right behind them. It was late evening when the plane took off, and after they were airborne the pilot turned off the cabin lights. Except for the odd overhead light, under which someone was reading, most of the passengers were trying to sleep as best they could. They all wanted to be as fresh as possible upon arrival in Ireland in the morning. Adam was trying to doze off, but it wasn't happening for him. Perhaps it was the excitement of the trip, but sleep wouldn't come.

He got up to use the rest room, and when he did, he got quite a shock. Hans and Barry had covered themselves with a blanket.

Barry was leaning back in his seat. His eyes were closed and he was moaning slightly. Hans was invisible. The blanket completely covered him. It took Adam a few seconds to realize that Hans was giving Barry a blow job. He decided to stand in the aisle, blocking their row, in case someone else should come by and see what was going on.

Barry began to make loud noises so Adam leaned over and put his hand over Barry's mouth. Barry opened his eyes in alarm. He realized what was happening, smiled at Adam, and muffled his own noises. Adam stayed there until Hans came up for air. Hans leaned over to Barry to kiss him, obviously sharing Barry's cum with him. They both smiled at Adam. Only then did Adam proceed to the rest room.

At the rear of the plane one of the flight attendants was reading a magazine. Adam asked if she could give him a blanket. She produced one quickly from one of the overhead compartments. When he returned to his seat, Evan was still dozing. He put the blanket over them and put his hand on Evan's crotch.

Evan stirred. He looked at Adam and smiled as he put his hand on Adam's crotch. They helped each other take their cocks out and they started stroking one another. Evan whispered to Adam, that the end was near so Adam ducked under the blanket and took Evan's spunk into his mouth, swallowing all of it. When he recovered, Evan did the same to Adam. They both failed to notice that Hans and Barry were standing in the aisle attempting to hide their activities. When finally the four sets of eyes met, they all laughed and Hans and Barry returned to their seats.

"I think that makes us all members of *The Mile High Club.*" Evan whispered to Adam as he dozed off once again.

———

Jim began to stroke Adam's cock in earnest, and Adam was awakened from his reveries. He started to do the same thing to Jim. They came seconds apart, bravely muffling the sounds of their passion. They used the blanket to clean themselves and then folded the blanket with the jism on the inside. They put the clean side of the blanket behind their heads and used it for a pillow. They dozed off, joining their travelling companion in the window seat, who continued to sleep peacefully for most of the flight.

Billy met them at the airport. "We'll have to take a convoluted route to your house, but I'm pretty familiar with which streets are open and which are closed. At first you never knew thanks to one after shock after another, but thank God, the tremors have finally stopped."

"Have all our utilities returned and what about mail?" Jim asked.

"Yes," Billy answered. "We have gas and electricity. Land line phone service was the first utility we got back, but we didn't start to get mail until a few days ago. I've been taking yours into the house and it's on the kitchen table. I'm expecting you for dinner tonight. You can go shopping tomorrow, but expect long lines and scanty shelves at the super market."

"Will Juan be there?" Adam asked.

"No, he's out of town on business. He's planning on importing exotic plants from Asia and he's there now making arrangements. You guys will have to settle for a threesome. I hope you aren't too tired."

"Shit!" Jim said. "We got each other off on the plane, and at our age, twice in one day is a dream that won't come true."

Billy laughed. "You old hound dogs, you," he said. "You should know by now that an orgasm isn't the be all. It's the end all. Kissing, caressing, cuddling and fondling are so much more fun. We'll just play, if that's cool with you."

"It's cool," Adam said.

"It's very cool." Jim echoed.

Billy dropped them off and said that he was going home to prepare supper, so they entered the house cautiously to assess any damage. The kitchen was neat and clean but they opened the cabinet doors to see what lay behind. Everything seemed to be Ok until they opened one cabinet which was completely empty. It had contained dinner plates and salad plates. They found a note inside in Billy's handwriting.

> *The door must have come open and all the plates spilled out. I cleaned up the mess, but I couldn't salvage a single plate. Put new dishes on your shopping list. I think you'll find the rest of the house intact. I turned over your car motor several times so you have no excuses for not coming to dinner tonight, whenever tonight will be. Billy*

Billy roasted a chicken with baked potatoes and green peas for dinner. It was simple but tasty and more than filling. Fred called during dinner and they all spoke to him. When Fred spoke to Adam, he lowered his voice and said, "Juan is out of the country. Take good care of my boy will you?"

Adam answered, "You bet I will."

They all pitched in with the dishes and with cleaning up the kitchen. Afterwards they watched television for a while. "It's nice to have TV back," Billy said. "We were without it for more than two weeks."

Adam took a moment to call Russ to let him know that they were home safely and enjoying dinner at Billy's. "Do everything I would do," Russ said laughing.

When Billy felt it was time, he turned off the set and said, "Enough TV. It's fun time." He headed for the bedroom with Jim and Adam following closely.

"Stay the night," Billy said. "You can go shopping tomorrow straight from here."

The three of them undressed and snuggled tightly in Billy's king size bed. Billy's erection was poking Adam's ass cheeks.

"I may not cum again today," Adam said, "but I'd have no objection to getting fucked."

"I'm ready for you guys," Billy said, and he opened his bedside table's drawer and extracted a tube of KY jelly. He greased both his guest's asses and his cock and began to fuck them alternately. When he could no longer restrain himself, it was Jim who was lucky enough to receive Billy's juices. They cleaned themselves up and got back in bed, cuddling close and fondling each other.

"I love you both," Billy whispered as he started to fall asleep."

"We love you," Adam whispered back.

The next day after breakfast at Billy's house, Adam and Jim drove cautiously to one of the many AID's charities' thrift shops which had sprung up all over the city. They found a nice set of dishes there and purchased it. Then they went to the Ralph's supermarket closest to their home and purchased what they needed to restock their refrigerator and pantry.

When everything was in place, they finally had a chance to relax. It was early morning on the east coast and they knew that Jamie and Tim would be awake by now. They called to fill them in on how they had found things. They made them laugh when they described sex on the plane, and they made them jealous when they told them that Billy fucked them last night.

"Maybe we'll come down before next August," Tim said.

"You're always welcome," Adam responded.

It was an exceptionally lovely day and Jim and Adam were relaxing on their back porch, reading the paper when the phone rang. They had an extension on the porch and Jim picked it up. He looked at the caller ID and smiled. "Hi Russ," he said. "What's cooking?"

"Great news," he said. "There are some problems in my LA office which were caused by the earthquake, and they are sending me out to trouble shoot. I'll be there for at least two weeks, and my wife, Maggie wants to come along. She's dying to meet my family in LA. Is there any chance we could stay with you? It'll kill me not to have sex with you guys, but it would be great just to be together and share my free time with you all."

"You gotta be kidding even to ask," Jim answered. "When will your asses be arriving?"

"The day after tomorrow. Our flight gets in at 10 AM. We'll rent a car and get right over. Tell Adam to get his memory cells in gear. Maggie wants to know all about Evan. Tell him to skip the sexy parts but keep them in mind for me."

"Will do!" Jim said. "But you've got to tell Maggie that we are gay and that your father was too. She has to be prepared before you get here."

"I've already told her and that has just added to her fascination over everything that has transpired."

"That's wonderful. I love you," Jim said as he hung up.

"I heard," Adam said. "How great is that? We'll not only have Evan's son staying in the house. But his wife as well. Hallelujah!!!" Adam looked like he was about to cry. Jim put his arms around him and Adam did indeed sob in his shoulder.

"God, how I wish I had Russ as a tot, so I could have raised him and seen him grow to manhood," Adam said. "Evan and I talked about adopting, but you can't do that in Florida to this day. We even discussed paying for a surrogate mother, but we never did. I think that if little Billy wasn't over at our house more than he was at home, we might have been more affirmative about it. I can't tell you how much it means to me knowing that I can hold Evan's natural son in my arms."

"I can well imagine," Jim said.

Adam and Jim spoke at great length about how they should greet Maggie. Should they just shake her hand until they all knew each other better or should they show a little more affection? In the end they concluded that Russ had told her that Adam was his surrogate father so they should give her a hug, and if she was receptive, a peck on the cheek. They agreed to hug Russ, but not to kiss him. They couldn't believe what a dilemma a simple greeting was turning out to be.

When they saw Russ's rental arrive in their driveway, they both became extremely nervous. They went outside to greet them and to help them with their luggage. Russ introduced them to Maggie and they each hugged her. She was the one who kissed them both on the cheek. Then they went to hug Russ. To their great surprise, he kissed them both lightly on the lips.

There were two large suit cases and two carry-ons in the trunk and everyone helped unload the car. They brought the cases upstairs to the guest room.

Hang your stuff up and please use the dresser drawers. When you freshen up, please come downstairs. We'll have lunch ready," Adam said. He and Jim went downstairs.

Alone in their room, Maggie said, "This is the most exciting thing that has ever happened in our lives. I am so happy for you, my darling. I can't imagine how you felt when you found out that louse was not your father, and that your real father was a wonderful man, a hero to boot."

"I cried," Russ freely admitted. Maggie gave him a big hug.

Over lunch, Maggie insisted on hearing how Adam and Evan met. "Are you sure you won't be embarrassed?" Adam asked innocently.

"Heavens no. You forget, when I met Russ, he was living with two mothers."

Adam laughed. "Yes, I did forget," he said. He started a short and sweet narrative. "I thought Evan and I met accidently in a gay bar near the university, but after he died I found his journal. The old scoundrel had been following me around. He planned our meeting the whole time."

Maggie smiled. "That is so totally romantic. How wonderful. Too bad you had to find out after he died. By the way that isn't so different from how Russ and I met. We were freshman in college, and before we ever met, he had his eyes on me. The lout actually dated my roommate so he could meet me. How sad is that."

"It sounds like you were very shy Russ," Jim said.

"I was," Russ answered and looked knowingly at Jim and Adam.

"Listen," Adam said. "Tonight we are taking you out to dinner, and no fighting over the tab. Tomorrow when you go to work, Russ, we are going to take Maggie sightseeing, and to Rodeo Drive so she can spend some of your hard earned money. How does that sound?"

"Like a terrific plan, except for spending my money," Russ laughed.

———————

In every city they visited in Europe, Hans, Barry, Evan and Adam hired a cab to take them sightseeing. At the end of the tour, they consulted their gay guide to the city and the driver dropped them off at a gay restaurant and bar. At most of these places they had a nice dinner, chatted with a few of the other patrons, who were anxious to practice their English, and that was that. Only in Rome did they get invited to a sex orgy. In the other cities they returned to their hotel and made their own little orgy. To be honest, the ordinary tourist sightseeing was more exciting than any of their visits to gay establishments.

———————

Riding around Los Angeles, Maggie was more interested in hearing about Evan, than in the sightseeing. It was only when they were strolling on Rodeo Drive that her interest peaked. She examined the windows of the outrageously expensive shops and to her credit, she declared that everything was too expensive. She enjoyed window shopping, but refrained from any purchasing.

They had lunch at a nice little café on The Drive and suddenly Maggie expressed an interest in hearing about how Evan's parents reacted when he came out to them.

"Very badly, I'm afraid," Adam sighed. "They kicked him out, and never had anything to do with him after that. His brother Eddie was the only one who accepted him and who stayed in touch. Fortunately we were already planning to move to Miami, and my folks adopted him. They insisted he call them Mom and Dad."

"How sad," Maggie said. "You're folks sound like wonderful people, Adam. I wish I could have known them."

"Well, you will meet my adopted son Billy tonight. His folks were even greater. They actually made a party to introduce Billy's partner to all their friends. They were proud of both of them, and now Fred is a State Senator. Lucky for us, he's home for a few days and he's joining us for dinner. By the way, since Billy and Russ both think of me as their father, they have become good friends and think of themselves as brothers."

"I know," Maggie said. "He told me." I think that it is fantastic that after all these years, Russ has a real father, a brother and a whole new family. I cry with joy every time I think about it."

Jim could no longer contain himself. "It doesn't bother you then that Russ's new family is all gay."

"Oh Jim, shame on you for asking me that. You have all made my husband so happy. I can't thank you enough, and anyway, it's nobody's business who falls in love with whom. I can tell from just talking to you men how much Adam and Evan loved each other, and how much you and Blake loved each other. Now you have found love again, and it makes me so happy for both of you."

Jim took Maggie's hand and squeezed it. "Thank you for that, Maggie. It means a lot to both of us to hear you say that. Now let's all go to the Beverly Center where prices are more reasonable, and we can all do a little shopping."

That evening *the family* went to a wonderful little bistro on Third Street. It was not a gay restaurant, but there were always a lot of gay men and women there and a good many straight patrons as well.

Maggie remarked that she and Russ never had an opportunity to break bread with his family. It was only something they did with hers. "I can't tell you all how wonderful it is to meet you and to be a part of your, no Russ's, family."

Billy added, "It's a pleasure to welcome you to the family, Maggie." He raised his glass in a mock toast. Everyone else did the same. Russ put his arm around Adam's shoulder and squeezed it.

Russ was so anxious to have sex with the guys that he worked out a plan. He bought Maggie a day at a spa. He dropped her off at the spa that day and went to work, but he left early and rushed back to Adam and Jim. Fred had returned to Sacramento and Billy was at work, so they couldn't join them. For two hours, the three men sucked each other to orgasm, but not before Russ fucked Adam and Jim without allowing himself to cum again. After they showered, Russ drove off to pick up Maggie while Jim and Adam prepared dinner.

They were sitting on the back porch basking in the late afternoon sun, when Maggie and Russ returned. Maggie looked refreshed and her face was glowing. "It was wonderful," she announced. "Thank you so much darling," and she kissed Russ on his cheek. "And did all you men have a good day?" she asked.

"Yes, it was a fantastic day," Jim said with a grin on his face.

Russ completed his work a few days earlier than expected, and he and Maggie flew home ahead of schedule. Everyone was sad to see them leave, but Russ said that he would be back in two weeks.

"We'll look forward to it," Adam said.

CHAPTER FIFTEEN

When Russ said that he would be back in two weeks, an obsessive thought invaded Adam's brain. Although it was true that Jim and Adam had established a relationship before Russ was in the picture, it was also true that the sexual activity between them had always been an event for three or more. Adam began to dream about having a night alone with Russ. He was so much like Evan that Adam longed to relive those intimate moments he and Evan had so lovingly shared. Right or wrong, he believed that Russ would be the vehicle through which his dreams might come true. He became so obsessed with the idea that he dared to approach Jim and ask if he would mind. He also reminded Jim that Monday was his eighty fifth birthday.

"I guess I can live for a night without sex, that is cuddling and fondling at least, but I'm just afraid that you will be disappointed. After all, Russ isn't Evan and even he can't bring Evan back to you. I'm afraid that you will inadvertently hurt yourself emotionally, but

I do think it's worth a try if it's all right with Russ. Besides you can figure to count that as one of my birthday presents to you." he said.

Adam gave Jim a great big hug and thanked him for his understanding. In the time remaining for Russ's visit, he was particularly attentive to Jim's sexual needs. Jim was happy to reap the benefits of allowing Russ and Adam to have play time without him.

They waited dinner for Russ's arrival on Sunday evening. During dinner Jim said, "Russ, Adam has something he wants to ask you."

"Shoot!" Russ responded, looking quizzically at Adam.

Adam found it difficult to explain the emotional need he had to try to relive his intimacy with Evan, but after a lot of faltering he was able to explain his need and how Russ could help. As Russ began to grasp Adam's yearning, his obsession, he began to sob. He embraced Adam and held him close.

"Of course, I'm willing, but I don't want to slight Jim. I love him so much also. How about this? I'll be in LA until Wednesday afternoon. How about I sleep with you tonight, Jim tomorrow night and we all share a bed Tuesday night." They all loved the idea and drank a toast to it.

After dinner, they watched TV awhile until Russ sensed that Adam was getting fidgety. "Let's turn in Adam," he said with a wink.

"I'll hang out here for a while," Jim said. Adam and Russ got up and each kissed Jim. As he kissed his partner, Adam said, "Thank you darling."

The two men agreed to sleep in the guest room that night and went to what was hardly the guest room anymore. It had become Russ's bedroom. He had even begun to leave articles of his clothing there, so that he could travel lighter.

Adam took Russ's hand and they sat down on Russ's bed. "If I call you Evan while we are making love, please understand," Adam explained.

"No problem," Russ assured him.

"I'm going to ask you to participate with me and do whatever Evan and I used to do. Is that OK with you?"

"Absolutely!"

Adam leaned into Russ and began to kiss him. Russ readily responded and kissed back. Slowly their kisses became more passionate. Adam began to unbutton Russ's dress shirt. He had already removed his tie before dinner. Russ allowed Adam easy access and started to pull Adam's polo shirt over his head. It didn't go smoothly but in a little while they were both topless.

Adam leaned over and began to nibble on one of Russ's nipples. He was pleased to notice that Russ was as hard and lean as his father. There would be no love handles tonight. Russ began to undo Adam's belt so Adam did the same for Russ. Now they both stood up and removed the rest of their clothing by themselves. Russ had a really hard erection, but, of course, Adam was only slightly engorged.

"What did Evan do next?" Russ asked.

"He laid me gently on the bed on my back and climbed on top of me. As big and strong as he was, I never felt his weight. He would rub our cocks together and kiss me passionately."

Russ did what his father had done. As he kissed Adam his cock ground hard against Adam's. Adam could feel Russ's cock twitching. Russ wanted (needed?) more. "What next?" Russ mumbled.

"Evan would slither down my body. He would kiss my neck, my ears, and my nipples. His tongue would caress my belly and my pubic area. We both shaved clean. I haven't shaved there in years, but I did for tonight. Before he would touch my balls or my cock, he would roll me over and rim me. When I was crying for mercy, he would roll me on my back again and gobble up my cock. He learned over the years to take all of me inside. When he felt that I was nearing orgasm, he would stop and ask if I wanted to cum in his ass or in his

mouth. I always varied my answer and he would accommodate me.
I can't enter you Russ darling so it will have to be in your mouth."

Russ didn't say anything, but he began to do everything Adam
had described. He was much more adept at nibbling on Adam's
nipples than Evan had been. When Adam mentioned that to Russ,
Russ laughed and said, "Don't forget, I've been nibbling on a woman's
nipples for years."

Russ continued to lick Adam all over. When he began to rim
Adam, he moaned so loudly, Russ was afraid he was cumming, so he
turned him over and took Adam into his waiting, hungry mouth.

Sometimes an orgasm would almost sneak up on Adam. He
would feel it coming on and instantly he shot his load. Other times, his
orgasm would build and build, happening slowly, and then overwhelm
him with intensity. Tonight was such a night. Adam felt his orgasm
building and building until finally it arrived and he had to scream out,
"I'm cumming, Evan. I'm cumming." Russ was prepared for Adam
to call him Evan.

Adam's octogenarian body produced very little semen. Russ
hardly tasted it, and he swallowed whatever little was produced.

For a while they lay side by side while Adam recovered.
Then Adam rolled on top of Russ. Again their cocks rubbed together.
Adam was flaccid, but Russ was hard as the proverbial rock. Adam
began to lick the inside of Russ's ear. Maggie and Jim never really
licked him there. His whole body shivered as an electric feeling went
through him.

"Oh God, Adam," he moaned.

"Do not use my name in vain," Adam joked as he slithered
further down Russ's body. Adam repeated every move he had ever
performed on Evan. He lingered especially long when rimming Russ.
Russ was not about to stop him, but when Adam sensed that Russ
was in great need of cumming, he stopped rimming and took a tube

of lube from the bedside table. He lubed his twitching ass and Russ's throbbing cock. "Fuck me, please," he begged Russ.

Russ entered Adam as slowly as he could. He began to stroke even slower. He was in no hurry and Adam appreciated it. He dreamed that Evan was inside of him once again, uniting their bodies into a spiritual and sexual union. His tears began to flow. He was lying on his back and Russ began to kiss Adam's tears, drying his face. While he stroked in and out of Adam, Russ and Adam kissed passionately. Their tongues dueled hard, trying to get far down the other's throat. Adam thought that he might die of sheer happiness, but vowed to live so that he and Russ could repeat this night many times in the future.

When Russ's juices filled Adam's insides, he cried out in ecstasy, "Oh Evan, I love you so much." Russ was in no way insulted. He responded by kissing Adam even more passionately.

They took a quick shower together and returned to bed. They cuddled, kissed and fondled each other. Just before he fell asleep, Adam said, "I'm sorry Russ for calling you Evan."

"Nonsense, you honor me."

It was Adam's fortieth birthday, and he took the day off. In fact, every employee of his firm was given the day off on his birthday. He woke early that morning. It was still dark outside. He nudged his sleeping partner and when Evan became aware of his surroundings, Adam said, "Fuck me before you go to work. It'll be a birthday present."

"I have a whole evening of goodies planned, but your wish is my command."

Evan started to get out of bed, but Adam stopped him. "I don't care about morning breath or lubrication. Just fuck me, raw and hard."

Evan did just that and Adam was very turned on by the overlapping pain and the pleasure. He came a second before Evan. When it was over, they showered together and Evan ran off to work. Adam went back to bed to enjoy another couple of hours of pure idleness.

Finally, he had enough of this hedonism and he got up to dress. When he opened their walk in closet, Adam spied a pair of trousers lying on the floor. It must have slipped off the hanger. He recognized it as the pair Evan had warn to an office party the previous Saturday evening. Naturally he did not attend. As far as Evan's office was concerned, there was no Adam Langston.

He retrieved the trousers and folded it in preparation of hanging it up again. As he did so a slip of paper fell out of one of the pockets. Adam hung up the trousers and then picked up the paper. He unfolded it and read: *Evan, you were fantastic the other afternoon. When can you get away again? Call me soon: 305-444-7862. Terry.*

Adam was stunned, but not surprised. He long suspected Evan's infidelity. He had always believed that monogamy was not part of Evan's philosophy. The strange thing was that it didn't bother him. He knew that Evan's infidelity stemmed from lust, not love. Evan loved him and he loved Evan and that was all that mattered. Certainly Evan never avoided sex with him. He had plenty of sexual stamina to keep Adam satisfied. So he kept his mouth shut and pretended not to notice.

Adam vaguely remembered meeting someone named Terry at a Memorial Day party at the GLCC. Evan had introduced him as one of his co-workers. They had previously seen each other in a gay bar. They spoke briefly at the bar, and agreed to keep their secret at work in order to protect their careers. Adam's recollection of Terry, if it was the same Terry, was hot, very hot. He couldn't blame Evan at all.

He knew that Terry would be at work, but on a lark he decided to dial Terry's number. Imagine his surprise when a voice answered, "Terry Williams, here," the voice said. Adam nearly hung up, but he was suddenly possessed." Hi Terry," he said. "You probably don't remember me, but I'm Adam, Evan Morrissey's partner. I really didn't expect to find you at home."

There was a long silence. After a few seconds, while Terry regained his composure, he said, "Why yes, I remember you well. I remember thinking how cute you were. I think I can guess why you are calling. You found out about Evan and me, didn't you?"

Terry sounded distraught so Adam said. "Be cool, chum, I don't mind at all. In fact I have the day off, and Evan won't be home until six. He told me what a great lover you are. I thought maybe you'd like to come over and show me."

"That's a hard invitation to refuse," Terry said. "I'm home because I'm leaving on a business trip to New York at 5 PM this evening. I can be packed and ready in fifteen minutes and that will give us plenty of time."

"How did you intend to get to the airport?" Adam asked.

"By cab."

"Then I have a better idea. I'll drive to you, and later I can get you to the airport, and save you the cab fare."

Terry said, "That's great. I live at 623 Sycamore St. in Miami. Do you know where that is?"

Adam didn't know, so Terry gave him directions. "I can be there in a half hour," Adam said. "Be ready for me."

"You bet," Terry said. "Hurry!"

When Adam arrived and Terry let him into the front hall, he saw a suitcase and a carry on lying on the floor in the hall. Terry was wearing a bathrobe. Adam assumed that there was nothing on underneath. As soon as he closed the front door, Terry grabbed Adam and began to kiss him. Adam was right. Terry had nothing on except the robe. Adam kissed Terry back, passionately. His mind was racing a mile a minute, but his cock was also rising. *What's sauce for the goose is sauce for the gander,* he thought. *Screw you Evan.*

Right there in the hallway, Adam fell to his knees, pulled the robe apart and engulfed Terry's cock in his mouth.

"Wow," Terry said. "That was fast and unexpected. Let's get into my bed."

For two hours they made wild and kinky love. They even fucked in the bath tub. They had admitted to each other that it was a favorite thing of both of them. Terry was a hungry bull. He came twice in Adam's mouth, and once in Adam's ass. Adam was sore from Evan fucking him that morning without lubrication, but he gritted his teeth and took it.

Neither exhibited one moment of tenderness. It was raw, primal sex and that's what each wanted. When they were spent, they lay in bed kissing and fondling each other while they both recovered.

"Don't tell Evan," Terry said, "but you are a way better lover than he is."

"I won't tell for sure, and you are even better than he described," Adam lied. "Also I would appreciate if you didn't tell Evan about us. He cheats on me, but he's very jealous if I cheat on him."

"Then it's our secret," Terry agreed.

On the way to the airport, Terry asked, "Do you think when I get back that we can do this again?"

"We'll see," Adam answered, knowing that it would never happen.

He got home in plenty of time to shower and change before Evan came home. They greeted each other warmly and then Adam asked, "Where are you taking me for dinner on my fortieth birthday?"

"You'll see. I have a surprise."

They arrived at a four star restaurant in North Miami. "Damn," Adam said, "this will cost you a fortune."

"You're worth it, love."

A shout of "SURPRISE!" invaded Adam's ear drums. When he could focus he recognized the Binghams and the Richters. Sarah looked terribly ill. She was ashen, and Ben was practically holding her up. Suddenly Adam was tackled from behind by Barry and Hans. They smothered him with hugs and kisses. When things settled down, Jack Bingham said that Billy had sent love from school, and said that he was sorry that he couldn't be there.

"Even though he isn't here," Jack said. "Let's make this a birthday you'll never forget, Adam."

"I assure you," Adam said. "I'll always remember this one."

EPILOGUE

Jim made Adam a ninetieth birthday party. Jamie and Tim flew in from Ft. Lauderdale. Also present were Billy, Fred, Juan and Jonathan plus a pitiful few of Adam's friends. In the seven years Jim and Adam had been together, they had lost at least a dozen friends to natural causes. Adam was becoming depressed. The most pleasant surprise of the day was that Russ attended with his wife.

When Maggie had accompanied Russ on his two week business trip to LA following the earthquake, he revealed to her, in advance of the trip, that his biological father had been gay and that Adam had been his partner since they were college freshman. Of course he neglected to tell her about his own sexual involvement. She thought nothing of it, and she was anxious to meet Adam. After all he had shared his life with Russ's father and she felt that she and Russ should share their lives with him.

Jamie and Tim were staying with Billy and Fred because Maggie and Russ had arrived the night before and Jim insisted that they stay with him and Adam. They had dinner together that night and Maggie plied Adam for even more stories about Evan. She was totally fascinated by the events which had revealed to Russ his true origins. Adam was delighted to talk about Evan and their life together. Russ grew more and more proud that Evan had been his father.

At some point, Adam excused himself and went to his room. He took a small box out of a dresser drawer and returned to the dinner table. He handed Russ the box.

"What is this?" Russ asked.

"Open it up and you will find a bullet in it. When Evan was wounded in France, the doctor's left one bullet in him. It was too close to his heart to risk removing. When he died, I asked the mortician to remove it and give it to me. I think that you should have it now."

A tear came to Russ's eyes.

"This is a great honor," he said to Adam.

The party was very successful and lots of fun. Jim roasted Adam unmercifully. When it was over, Jim drove Jamie and Tim and Maggie and Russ to the airport to make their flights home. Adam was too tired to accompany him and besides there was no room in the car.

Alone in the house, Adam walked slowly to his bedroom. He wanted to shower but he was too exhausted. He undressed fully as was his habit, and lay down in bed. He pulled the covers over him and fell asleep.

In his sleep he clearly heard Russ calling him, but he realized that Russ had left the house. Adam smiled. It wasn't Russ at all. It was Evan. Adam awoke and sat up in bed.

There was Evan standing at the foot of the bed. He was naked and very young. His body was aglow and he held out his arms to Adam.

Adam got out of bed and approached Evan. They held out their arms to each other and embraced. A warm glow went through Adam's body.

"I love you," Evan said to him. "I will love you for eternity. Come home with me now. It's time."

Evan separated himself from Adam and took his hand. Adam could see a very bright light behind Evan's ghost and Evan was leading him toward that light. When Evan took Adam's hand he looked at their clasped hands and was amazed. His hand was young, without wrinkles and lines. He glanced in the bedroom mirror and saw a young version of himself, barely twenty years old.

He squeezed Evan's hand tighter and tighter, and allowed Evan to lead him into the light.

A Boner Book

ABOUT THE AUTHOR

Hank Brooks was born in Brooklyn, NY and lived most of his adult life in and around the New York City area.

He is very active in SAGE, a senior advocacy group for gay men and women.

He has three children and five grandsons. He is a retired CPA, and now lives with his partner, Leo, in Coconut Creek, Florida.

3 EROTIC GAY NOVELLAS

BY HANK BROOKS

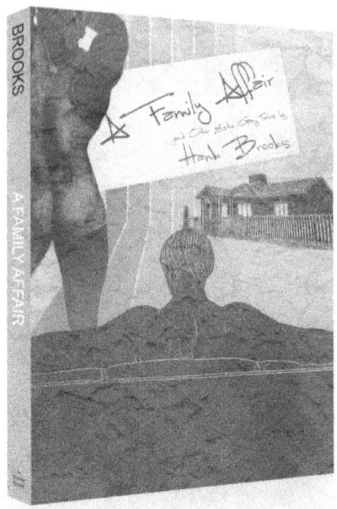

A FAMILY AFFAIR

FATHERS and SONS

a novel by HANK BROOKS

AN ANTHOLOGY OF EROTICA
Gay Love Stories

by HANK BROOKS

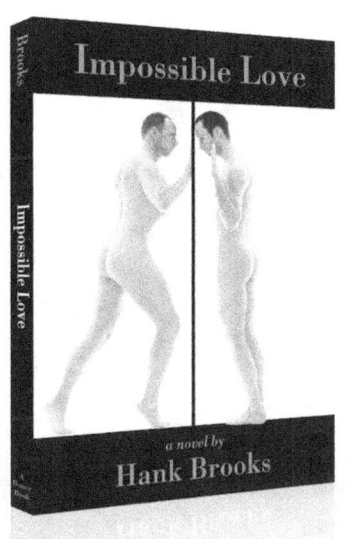

Impossible Love
Brooks
Impossible Love
a novel by
Hank Brooks

BROOKS
OBSESSION AND DECEPTION
OBSESSION AND
DECEPTION
HANK BROOKS

BROOKS
TALES OF RICK & ALEC
TALES OF RICK & ALEC
HANK BROOKS

BROOKS
the INLET
THE INLET
HANK BROOKS